Runaway to New York

Runaway Romance Series

Book 2

Misty Rosette

Copyright © Misty Rosette

This is a work of fiction. Names, characters, places, and incidents either are products of the author's imagination or are used fictitiously. Any similarity to actual events or locales or persons, living or dead, is entirely coincidental

CONTENTS

CHAPTER ONE

TWO WEEKS AGO

The phone notification chimed in the darkroom. Felicia groaned in her sleep, angry at the gadget for waking her up, but she reached for the phone in the drawer beside her bed. She felt the phone, picked it and brought it to her face.

Felicia saw she had two missed calls and three messages from Francisca, her sister. The upper part of her phone read Five A.M in the morning. It was very early. So why was Francisca calling her this early?

Rubbing the sleep out of her eyes with one hand, she opened the messages.

Francisca wrote in the first message: Please, I need you, Felicia. Francisca wrote the second message: I can't talk on the phone, can you come to the guest house? I have something to share with you. In the third and last message, Francisca wrote: I need to talk to you, or I am not sure about the wedding anymore!

Francisca was having second thoughts about her wedding?

Felicia quickly shook her head to dismiss the thought and got out of bed. She tried calling her sister, but she didn't pick up the call. So, Felicia ran out of the house to the guest house, which wasn't far from their main residence.

When Felicia got there, she met the entrance door slightly opened. She didn't think twice about it and ran inside thinking.

The only thought on her mind was how she would help Francisca. But as soon as Felicia entered the house, she knew that something was wrong. The place was eerily empty, and Francisca's phone was on a table in the living room.

Felicia felt her phone vibrating in her pocket and saw that Francisca's phone was calling hers. She gulped easily.

"Fran?" she asked in a shaky voice. "Are you here? Are you okay?"

A part of her mind already knew that she wouldn't get any answers, but that didn't mean that she was prepared for the silence that greeted her. She took a deep breath and realized that she might actually be acting paranoid and just be overthinking.

So, she ran up the stairs, searching all the three bedrooms in the house but couldn't find any sign of Francisca. Her whole body was shaking while her over-imaginative mind was thinking of different things that could have happened to her twin sister. When Felicia was a hundred percent certain that she was the only one in the house, she decided it would be better to call her father and tell him what happened.

But as she walked down the stairs towards the front, she heard the front door slam shut. She hurried in fear to the front door to try to open the door but noticed that there was a hose-like pipe under the locked door and a gas she didn't recognize was filling the room.

Felicia's eyes watered while her throat hurt and her whole body felt weak suddenly, she pulled herself up the stairs with everything she could muster, but her legs felt like jelly.

How was this happening? Was that psycho trying to kill her already? The police said that she was safe, so how did he enter their house to do this? No, this wasn't the time to think about this; she should be trying to save herself.

She pressed her number one button on her phone for the speed dial, but she could already feel herself under the spell of the gas. She heard the voice on the other end of the line and tried to find the words to convey her situation, but her tongue wouldn't form the words.

"Felicia? Can you hear me? ...tell me where you are," The voice pleaded.

Felicia could hear the urgency in the person's voice. So, she forced herself to muster the words.

"Guesthouse" She gasped and ultimately gave in to the darkness.

Was it being minutes later or hours later? The time was fuzzy. Felicia opened her eyes and saw her father, Felix, talking to two men on the other end of the room. She recognized the commissioner; Felicia had met him twice, but she couldn't see the face of the younger man. His back was turned to her.

"There is nothing we can do right now." The commissioner said, with clenched teeth and fists. "Felix, you have to convince your daughter. Tell her she has to leave London before that serial killer tries again|."

"She is not listening to me; she claims that she doesn't want to run!" Felix groaned, running his hand through his hair, frustrated.

The third man, Felicia couldn't see, leaned toward Felix. "Well, if you don't want her to lose her life, you will make sure that she leaves the country because that is the only way to save her life."

Felix blinked in shock, groaning in pain as he stared at his daughter. "I will do it. I will convince Felicia, and she will leave soon!

"That's the only thing we can do now, and I will also protect her," the third man promised.

Felicia smiled in her sleep. She wasn't a damsel in distress. Actually, she was the kind of person who prefers to face her fears head-on and protect herself by herself, but there was nothing wrong in letting a handsome man protect her, or is there?

How did you know he is handsome; you never saw his face? A little voice asked her. *You just know!* Came the mischievous reply.

***

"Aargh!" Felicia gripped the wheels so tightly her knuckles turned red as the feeling of anxiety overwhelmed her senses. Her father had coaxed her to leave London today because that was the only way she could stay safe and also because that would buy the police time while they tried to find the person trying to kill her.

She had had two near-death experiences, and the last one had seemed to scare her father to the point that he didn't listen to anything she had to say. Cried, telling him that she didn't want to run, but Mr. Felix Smith was beyond any type of reasoning, and Felicia couldn't blame the man. He was scared out of his mind.

Felicia groaned as tears threatened to fall down her face. She had lived all of her life in London, hardly traveled out of the country except a few times as a child. She had made plans for her future here, and everything had been going according to plan until now. At this moment, it feels like everything is crashing down around.

She loved her life here. London has this allure of simplicity layered in a sophisticated scenery filled with greenery at almost every turn, filled with history and stories at every landmark.

The people from different races and works of life all come together to make a bubbling and thriving city, and she didn't want to give it up, especially not for a stranger but her life's decision wasn't in her hands anymore. It was controlled by a psychopath's decision to ruin her.

She scoffed and clenched her teeth as she approached the second bend on her right leading on to Lambeth Bridge. The police told her that the best action would be to leave the country without telling anyone, but Felicia didn't want to run and hide. She had lived in London all her life. Felicia swallowed hard in her already dried mouth as she remembered the incidents within the last month. Francisca, Felicia's twin, returned like a prodigal daughter from Paris.

Felicia and Francisca might be identical twins, but they were as different as night and day. Where Francisca was a hot-headed, impulsive twin with a mind of her own, Felicia was calm, calculative, and too thorough when making any decision.

So, when Francisca had run away from her engagement ceremony because she didn't want an arranged marriage, no one was really surprised. After all, it was something Francisca would do.

The irony was Francisca's wedding was arranged because their father, Felix Smith, found out that a psychopath was after his daughter. A serial killer killed daughters from prominent families of marriageable age who weren't married.

The serial killer was called the 'Wedding psychopath' because he would print a grimly wedding invitation with the target name, send it to the victim's home, and then kill the victim within a few months if the victim did not get married within that time.

A new wave of anger hit Felicia when she remembered how the serial killer almost destroyed their family. Felix got the invitation with Francisca's name on it. He knew telling his hotheaded daughter to get married to save her life was out of the question, so he and his best friend Baron Saylor had arranged her engagement to his son, Charles, without Francisca's consent, without telling her the reason, and Francisca who didn't want to be tied to someone she barely knew…ran away from home.

Of course, Francisca came back a year later, engaged! The twist of fate was that she was engaged to Charles, the man she ran away from. It was a funny coincidence. Felicia had to admit that she liked Charles, her new brother-in-law. He was the perfect person for Francisca.

Francisca acted differently with Charles around. She was more focused, happier, and obviously in love. The two love birds didn't want to be apart from one another, so they married two weeks ago.

The whole family had felt complete. Just being back with each other made the hurts and the pain they felt in the past disappear like foam. That was until that stupid letter came. The happiness was short-lived; the 'Wedding psychopath' declared that Felicia was his next target!

Mad was an understatement of the turmoil boiling in Felicia's heart. All her life, she had been the good sister, the cool-headed daughter, the shoulder everyone relied on, but at this moment, she felt her life slipping through her fingers. There was nothing she could do to stop it from happening.

Her life was indirectly controlled by a psychopath trying to kill her because he wanted to fulfill an idea or fantasy about how she was supposed to live her life.

It was stuffing!

Over the past month, she and Francisca had gotten closer. They both have come to respect, love one another, and accept their individual differences. This was the time she was supposed to spend with her family. This wasn't the time for her to run away.

Felicia reached for her phone in her Louis Vuitton bag and dialed Francisca's number.

Ring, Ring!!!

The line ran three times before someone picked up the call.

"Hello?" Felicia said excitedly.

"Felicia?" Francisca's warm voice came clearly over the line. "You left without saying goodbye!"

Felicia laughed softly as tears filled her eyes. "I was told that it was better not to talk to anyone before I left for the airport."

Felicia could hear Francisca sniffing.

"Are you crying?" Felicia asked her headstrong twin.

"Wait, you mean me? Nope. I am not crying," Francisca denied vehemently. "I have the flu, that's all."

Felicia smiled to herself. She knew her sister more than Francisca would have liked. Felicia knew that her sister would never admit to being soft. Still, Felicia knew that she was one of the softhearted people she had ever met in her life.

"I believe you," Felicia added. She wasn't about to bruise Francisca's ego. "How is the husband, and how is married life?" She continued.

"Well-" Francisca paused dramatically. There was a smile in her voice. "The husband is sexy as he can be, and I am taking the marriage life one day at a time."

"Huh-uh"

"I wish you could open your heart and see that love is a beautiful thing," Francisca said.

Felicia smiled. It wasn't long ago that Francisca said she would never marry or fall in love. After getting married to Chris, she has become a loving advocate and does everything to convince people that love is superb and everyone must have a taste of it.

"Are you sure you don't own a dating agency, site, or something?" Felicia teased.

"You are so funny," Francisca chided. "But I wish I could convince you to stay, but I can't even do that because you will be safer if you leave."

Felicia could hear the change in her sister's voice, and she ground at teeth in anger. Someone was causing pain to her family, but whoever that psycho was, he was sleeping peacefully while tearing her family apart.

"Fran, listen to me" Felicia paused. "In the end. I made the final decision to leave," Felicia convinced warmly.

Felicia made a quick swerve to her left to avoid the Lamborghini speeding past her, and her heart skipped a beat. There was something wrong! Her heart stopped beating for a second too long, and her brain didn't want to believe what was happening. Felicia stepped on the break again, but nothing happened. She gasped in shock as her bottom lips wobbled of their free will. She swallowed hard and tightened her hands on the steering wheel.

Why was this happening? Her heart broke anew. Wasn't the universe tired of throwing stones in her path?

"Felicia, is everything fine?" Francisca asked.

Felicia glanced at the phone, back at the road, and a drop of tear fell down her face. The last person she would talk to before she dies is Francisca? Francisca shook her head frantically. No! The universe might try to take from her, but she won't let her sister hear her screaming to her death.

"I'm sorry, Fran," Felicia said as gently as she mustered.

"What?" Francisca's voice shook over the phone. She didn't know what was wrong with Felicia, but she could feel that something was wary. "Talk to me, Felicia. What is wrong?"

Felicia scoffed and shook her head as if Francisca could see her. "Nothing, I was just missing you. That's all."

"Are you sure?" Her voice didn't sound convinced.

"Of course, so hang up the call and say hi to Chris for me," Felicia added with a short laugh.

"Of course, I will do that. Just stay safe. Huh?"

"Bye, I love you," Felicia added and hanged up before Francisca spoke again.

Felicia couldn't remember when it was the last time she told

Fran that she loved her. Felicia knew that if she never said it today, she would never be able to say it ever because today was the day she died.

Suddenly waves of regrets hit her. There were thousands to a million things she wished she had done differently. She wished she had fallen in love; taken the executive position her father had offered. Felicia had turned it down because she didn't want to hurt Francisca, who didn't even care about the family business. She wished for many things, but she couldn't do anything about those wishes.

"Oh, God, I don't want to die," Felicia cried as she swerved from the blue Lexus, coming straight at her. The man who drove the Lexus rolled down his window and threw some words in Spanish at Felicia. She didn't need a translator to know that the man was cursing her, but she wasn't bothered by his words.

Instead, she focused on her driving as if her life depended on it because it did.

How could this have happened when the cops gave her the car so it wouldn't be tracked? How did the brakes suddenly quit working? With a shake of her head, she dismissed the idea. This wasn't the time to speculate on what had happened. Felicia took a deep breath and scolded herself.

If she could just find something, she could hit without also killing herself in the process. Felicia looked around her but couldn't find anything, she was on a bridge. She was on the Lambert Bridge. She could only go forward or backward, but she couldn't find anything to hit.

The loud sound of the horn coming snapped her out of reverie. Felicia saw the big trailer truck coming towards her. It was now or never. The only way out of this would be if she could drive this car into a ditch and jump out at the last second, but she wasn't Vin Diesel or a stuntman. There were limits to the actions she could make.

The truck approached her without swerving or switching lanes as if challenging her. Felicia used all of her effort to move the wheel to the right, paying close attention to the bridge's protective rail. She took her hands off the wheel and reached for the door, but something else was wrong...

The doors weren't opening. Felicia tried all the bottoms, all the buttons, kicked the door, but the doors didn't open. Her whole body shook frantically as her life flashed before her eyes. She knew she was going to die.

Her father's face and his sweet words of promise, telling her he would protect her and how her death would probably break him. Her mother's face gentle eyes, as she said goodbye to her even though she would rather hide her daughter in her bosom forever and Francisca...her twin would be fine. Felicia convinced herself as she braced herself for impact.

As the car fell off the bridge and into the water. Felicia cursed. She cursed the fate that gave her this life and took it without giving her a choice. Then the darkness enveloped everything she felt, but it wasn't peace she felt as she gave in to the feeling of nothingness.

It was despair.

Felicia felt anxious and helpless as life herself took the gift it had once given her as a young baby.

So, this was the end. This?

CHAPTER TWO

The tightness in Francisca's chest was not reducing, but she took a deep breath and cleared her throat as she paced around a spot. She was sure she heard wrong. That was her only conclusion.

"... I didn't get what you said, can you repeat it?" her voice shook; despite her bravado, her legs gave in under her, and she fell into the couch behind her. She dropped her phone!

She scoffed. Someone must be playing games with her because what she heard couldn't be true. So, she mustered her courage again and picked up the phone.

"Ma'am?" the female voice on the other end of the line asked gently.

"Yes, I am here. I think you have the wrong number," Francisca suggested calmly.

"Are you Francisca?" The voice continued patiently.

"Yes, but that doesn't mean-" Francisca added hastily.

"Your phone number was listed as an emergency contact on this phone. Also, you were the last person the deceased spoke to before the accident."

"Shut up," Francesca roared, standing up suddenly. "Stop saying deceased. My sister is not dead!"

Charles, Francisca's husband, had heard her voice, so he rushed to the living room where he saw Francisca shouting at her phone. He wasn't sure what had happened, but he was sure it wasn't anything good.

"What happened," he asked quickly.

Francisca turned slowly. Her face looked lost as she fell against Charles's chest while crying with her whole body.

"Baby, you have to speak to me. What happened? "He asked gently, putting his arm around her.

Francisca shook her head. "She kept lying. She keeps saying things that can't be true," her voice buried between his shirts.

Charles noticed the phone in Francisca's hand and that the call was still ongoing. He pried the phone gently from her hands and placed the phone to his ear.

"Hello, I heard that you are lying to my wife," Charles said softly.

Francisca raised her head to stare at Charles, whose body posture had tensed up suddenly. She glanced up at him with her eyes filled with dread but still filled with hope.

Charles didn't say a word but listened attentively to the lady on the other end of the phone. His face was pale, and he avoided looking at Francisca as much as possible. He only said the occasional "hmm" and "Ok" to the phone.

Finally, he ended the call, placed the phone gently on the table, and led Francisca back to the couch to sit. Then he kneeled in front of her and clasped her hand tightly in his.

'Babe, remember you are pregnant, and the doctor said that you should take things slowly?" Charles said as if he was pleading for understanding.

"Of course, I know that I am pregnant," she scoffed. "I am not a baby. I was on the phone with Felicia at the time, but I didn't tell her since I preferred to deliver her the happy news in person rather than over the phone."

"Baby…"

Francisca interrupted. "If you are going to tell me something that I don't want to hear, then don't say it" She shook her head vehemently, pleading with her eyes.

Charles's voice shook. "Just because you don't want to face something or deny that thing doesn't mean that it is a lie."

"I said stop!" she interrupted again, pushing him away, standing and hasty stepping away from him. "I don't want to hear it," she cried as tears fell down her face.

Her hands covered her ears. "I am not going to listen to you if you are just going to repeat what that woman said."

Charles's heart was breaking as he watched his wife crumbling right in front of him. He hurried over to her side and wrapped his arm around her tightly.

"Let me go. Stop all this, Felicia is fine" she tried to pull out of his embrace, but he was too strong.

"I am sorry, Fran," he cried as he tightened his arm around her.

Francisca hit him, throwing light punches on his back. "Stop saying sorry; Felicia is fine. I just spoke to her. She can't be dead!"

Francisca's leg gave out under her as soon as she said the word dead, and she let out a heart-wrenching scream that made Charles feel helpless. He gently went to the floor with her, his arms still around her as she cried out her heart.

"It is a prank. It is not real. No, it can't be true. Charles, tell me it isn't true!" she begged and cried.

"What happened here?" a familiar female voice asked behind them.

The couple jumped apart, and Chris's heart broke for the umpteenth time in the last hour. He didn't have to look up to know that the voice was his mother-in-law's voice, Chloe. He turned around and saw his father, Baron Saylor, and his in-laws staring at him and Francisca with questions in their eyes.

"You asked us to come, that you had a surprise for us. So, we all hurried over," Baron said softly. "So, what is going on? Why are you making her cry?

Chloe hurried over to her daughter and cleaned her tears with the tip of her sleeves. "Why are you crying like a baby? One would think you are a baby," Chloe said jokingly, but she sounded scared.

"I asked you a question. What happened here?" Baron asked again firmly in his low, no-nonsense voice.

Charles swallowed hard as he stared from Felix to Chloe. The words wouldn't form. From the corner of his eyes, he could see Francisca sniffling with hiccups as Chloe gently patted her shoulder.

"I don't know what happened, but it is going to be fine," Chloe assured. "Don't let things you can't change weigh you down!"

Francisca couldn't take it anymore. She threw her hands around her mother and cried. Her body breaking with every sob, Chloe looked up at Charles for an answer,

"What happened, Charles? Why is she crying?" Chloe asked.

"I-" Charles paused and swallowed. "I called you today because we found out that Fran was pregnant..."

Baron laughed. "Wow! That's joyous news" he knelt beside Francisca. "I know you are scared, but this is a good thing. I am going to be a grandfather."

Charles closed his eyes as a ragged breath escaped his lips. "But some minutes ago, we got a call from the police-"

He opened his mouth, but he couldn't find the word, everyone looked at him expectantly, but he didn't want to be the bearing of bad news, but he closed his eyes, opened them but lowered his gaze.

"They called and said Felicia was involved in a car accident. "He paused, cringing. "They said that she is dead!" Charles tumbled all the words quickly but didn't look at anybody after finishing.

"What did you say" Felix spoke for the first time since he entered the house. "Which police?"

Chloe pulled back from Francis so that she could look into her daughter's eyes. "What is the saying Francisca? What does he mean by the things he just said"?

"M-mum," Francisca's lips wobbled as she tried to catch her breath between sobs. "What are we going to do? It can't be true mum tells me it's not true."

Baron held Francisca's hands with a soft smile. "Of course, it is not true, dear. I am going to the police station now. I will find out what happened, so I need you to take a deep breath. Everything is going to be fine."

"It is a joke, right," Chloe said, running her hands through her hair in disbelief.

Felix grabbed Charles's collar. "I asked a question! I said, which police?"

"I just spoke to a friend at the police station," Baron said, taking off the phone from his ear.

Chloe rushed at Baron, out of breath. "...and what did he say?"

Baron swallowed. He didn't want to be the bearer of bad news either. He stared at the expectant faces in front of him. Even Francisca was looking at him with hope as she wiped her tear-stricken face with the back of her hand.

"What did he say, dad?" Charles asked again.

"The car Felicia was driving to the airport was indeed found at the bottom of the ditch. The car was driven off a bridge, and the body-" he paused, closed his eyes as a drop of tear fell down a side of his face. "The body found is a hundred percent match, but he wants her family to come and identify the body still."

A heart-wrenching scream escaped Chloe's lips as she fell to her knees to the ground. A desolate look of hopelessness replaced the tiny flicker of hope in Francisca's eyes, and she felt simply backward.

Charles rushed and caught Francisca's at the last minute before she could hit the floor. "Babe?" Charles shook her gently. "Wake up. Why are you doing this?"

"Blood" Chloe screamed and pointed at Francisca's leg.

"I will get the car," Baron said, hurting out of the house. "Let's get her to a hospital this instant."

"What is wrong with her" Charles froze. He couldn't move. He stood there looking at Francisca with a lost look.

"Wake up, you can't lose it right now" Chloe shook Charles. "Your wife needs you to be strong. Help her to the car now."

Charles snapped out of his funk, carried Francisca in his arms, and hurried out of the front door. Chloe followed closely behind them. When she got to the door, she realized that Felix was not following her.

"What's wrong? Aren't you coming?" She asked. "You are also not breaking down on me. Are you?"

Felix shook his head. "No, I want you to go to the hospital with Francisca. I will go to the police station and find out everything."

"Bu-"

Felix placed his palms gently on the sides of her face and forced a smile. "It is going to be fine. Don't overthink it. Think about your blood pressure. I will be with you soon."

Felix and Chloe headed for the door, and as they opened it. Chloe's voice gently asked. "You are going to bring our daughter home. Safe and sound, right?"

Felix squeezed her hand tightly. "Yes, I am bringing her home."

***

Two hours left, like two years. Within the time they had been waiting for the doctor's reports, Charles had grown ten years older. He shook his legs, impatiently waiting for news outside the operation theatre.

Baron didn't know how to comfort Charles, the boy was used to taking care of himself and not showing pain, but at this moment, he looked like he would break down at any given moment.

So, as a father, he did the only thing he could do. He sat beside Charles and clasped his son's hand tightly.

"Dad...if anything happened to Fran..." Charles choked on the last word, his whole body shaking as he broke into another round of sob.

Baron gently put his arms around Charles and hugged him, gently rubbing his back. Chloe also sat down beside Charles and patted his back gently.

"She is going to be fine," Chloe reassured, but it sounded more like she was trying to convince herself.

Outside the operation theatre, the indication light went out. A female doctor dressed in overalls emerged from the sliding door. The entire family hurried towards her with bated breath.

"I am Doctor Chen. I was in charge of Mrs. Francisca Saylor's operation," Chen, a Chinese in her thirties, stated gently.

"How is my daughter?" Chloe asked, looking as if she was about to break into a sob.

Doctor Chen smiled. "Mother and child are fine."

"Really?" Chloe grabbed Chen's hands; the other woman nodded as if she wasn't surprised by Chloe's behavior.

"There are no complications, but the patient is sleeping right now. You can check up on her in a few hours."

Charles's legs gave in under him, and he fell to his knees, his right hand on his chest. He cried as if his heart hurt, and it probably did. Baron and Chloe knelt beside Charles.

"You heard the doctor. Your wife and child are both fine," Chloe reassured.

"I heard...I know, but I was scared. I couldn't imagine my life without Fran," Charles cried.

"Well, you wouldn't have to," Baron chuckled.

Chloe saw him first. He ran towards the waiting room as someone had lost, but she didn't care, she ran towards him too and hugged him tightly.

"How is Fran?" Felix asked his wife, who was still hugging him tightly.

"She is fine," Chloe replied as she pulled back a little so that she could see his face. "What about Felicia?"

Silence.

Felix bit his bottom lip and attempted to speak, but tears streamed down his cheeks. Chloe let out a strained breath. He didn't have to say anything. He was looking at her, and she could see the answer in his eyes.

"She is dead, right," Chloe said as she plopped on the waiting bench behind her. For a second, Chloe didn't react. She rocked front and back for a while and suddenly broke into a cry and fainted against the chair she sat on.

Felix ran towards Chloe. "I am sorry, babe," he cried. "I am really sorry."

Doctor Chen dashed towards Chloe to help her. Felix stepped away from Chloe. His face filled with regret and pain as he stared at his whole family in distress. He wished he could do something to alleviate their pain, but there wasn't anything he could do.

Being a father shouldn't be this hard!

***

Ms. Felicia Smith was laid to rest today, the 25th of April, 2021... the headline of the sun written in big, bold letters on the front page. The man squeezed the paper tightly in his hands. His heart hurt, and it wasn't from the occasional banging noise coming from his neighbors, upstairs but it was this stupid piece of news.

This wasn't how it was supposed to happen. It was supposed to be perfect. Not like this. There was no beauty, art, or fulfillment in this death. Even the media was not talking about him, as if he wasn't the one who orchestrated the whole thing.

Everyone thinks it is just a simple break failure, but it wasn't. He had cut the wires when he found out that Felicia would run away, but he had not meant to kill her. He had thought that she could get hurt a little, making it easy for him to kidnap her and make her death beautiful.

Not, this …this inferiority that holds no meaning.

He plopped into the sofa behind him, picked the bottle of cold beer beside his chair, and brought the drink to his lips. He closed his eyes and slipped into a dreamlike world. Felicia, he remembered the first time he met her. She had been the absolute opposite of what he expected.

She smiled and called his name softly and even went as far as touching his elbow gently when he fell in front of her. She hadn't been like any of the other single girls. Her eyes seemed to speak into his soul whenever she stared at him, and his heart skipped a beat.

He even reminisced asking her out one time, but he shook his head. That would be wrong! No matter how angelic Felicia smith was. He knew he couldn't give her preferential treatment. If he did, then he would have broken the vow he made to himself.

All these girls would burn in hell at his hands.

He still remembered the first time he killed his first victim. The fear in her eyes, coupled with surprise. He was confident that she hadn't expected he would be the last face she would see before her death.

The first time he killed, it had been for revenge. The embarrassment that bitch gave him irked him to the core. How could she disgrace him? He loved her, and she knew it, but she had taken advantage of his feelings and made fun of him. Why? Just because she was rich?

He had come to realize how all women are. So, when he started teaching them a lesson. They understood their place, every single one of them. That was what papa always said when he was younger. Papa has said that a woman who didn't know her place was dangerous, and he was right.

Momma didn't know her place, and Papa had taught her a lesson. The 'Wedding Psychopath' he liked the name. It was time to stop brooding about Felicia's death, and it was time to pick his next unwilling bride or victim.

The woman can be anything she wants to be. It all depends on her and if she knows her place. He smiled to himself as the thought of a new prey crossed his mind. This time around, he would make sure that it was perfect.

There would be no more mistakes.

His unwilling brides don't realize that he is doing them a favor. The daughters of prominent families were getting married because of him. | He had killed just four of his unwilling brides, and Felicia would have been the fifth if she hadn't died pathetically!

Bang bang.

The man opened his eyes glared at the ceiling in anger. How many times would he warn them that a human being lives downstairs? He couldn't even dream of peace because of them. Why can't people be considerate like him?

He let out of breath he hadn't realized that he was holding when the noise stopped for a second. He relaxed back on the chair and closed his eyes once again, and Felicia's face appeared again in his head.

"Are you sure that you are fine? I think you hurt your arm when you fell," her gentle voice said as she stared into his soul.

He smiled at her and raised his hand to touch her face, but she disappeared, and he opened his eyes. A hint of regret and need seeped through his whole body, and he sighed bitterly.

The seven-pomp alarm on his phone buzzed loudly. The man stood up while adjusting his shirt. It is time to get and work. He will send his new unwilling bride a message soon.

***

Young couples stabbed to death… Chief Officer Daniel Ford threw the newspaper on the table with a violent thud, wagging his finger at the paper. He turned to face his subordinates, who stood straight with grim bowed faces.

"Another murder?" Daniel growled, pacing around a spot like a caged animal. "I look like a fool at the Commissioner because all this murder is occurring in my district!"

"We are working with the evidence we got from the site," Jerry, a superintendent, said.

"So, you're saying the murderer is smarter than the best of the best in my police force?" Daniel hit the table with a fist. "Because I don't understand why you haven't caught him."

A retort was building at the tip of Jerry's tongue, so he bit the inside of his cheek. Why didn't the commissioner just go out into the field to catch criminals instead of acting self-righteous behind safe doors if it was so easy?

Jerry felt a shadow in his face and realized that the commissioner was standing in front of him.

"I'm I so boring that you are falling asleep?"

Jerry shook his head quickly. "No, sir! I was thinking of the evidence we collected from the scene, and there were some disturbing facts."

"Spill It"

"The murdered knew what he was doing. This wasn't his first kill, and he didn't make any decision without thoroughly thinking about it…."

"And how does this help the case" Daniel growled, losing patience.

Jerry took a deep breath and closed his eyes. It was something he hadn't really noticed because this wasn't the 'Wedding Psychopath's M.O, but there was a signature at the site.

The bastard had left a mark that he was there.

Jerry felt a hand on his shoulder shaking him. He opened his eyes, chuckling nervously as he met the commissioner's gaze.

"Are you sleeping right now?" the man asked in awe.

"No, I figure out that the wedding Psychopath was the same person who killed the couple."

"Bu-but that isn't…."

"It is possible. It was the same killing method with the girls, and we never told the media how that bastard operates."

Daniel placed a hand on the back of his neck as if he had a sudden pain and plopped to the chair in despair.

"He is killing random people now?" Daniel glanced at the calendar on the opposite end of his office. He had a few months to retirement; this wasn't how he had expected to go!

Jerry smiled sheepishly. This case was becoming more interesting by the day!

CHAPTER THREE

The light from the bulb hurt her eyes as she tried to open it and her throat was also painful. How long has she been out? She asked herself as she blocked the ray of the light by putting her hands over her face.

When she finally opened her eyes, she saw that she was still in the hospital. The white walls and bedding with the subtle chlorine smell almost made her gag. Shouldn't she be lying down like this? She glanced at her arm and saw the IV attached to it. She groaned inwardly. As if she was saying, "Ah, I've found the culprit, causing my headaches." She pulled it out and leaned against the IV pole to get to her feet. It was hard, but her determination to get out of his room was intense.

A firm determination can get you anywhere, even if your legs feel like jelly, and that was exactly how she felt as soon as her feet hit the ground. A wave of dizziness hit her, but she shook her head. This wasn't the time to give in to the weakness she felt.

With legs that felt like wood, she dragged the pole to the door. One step at a time. When she got to the door and turned the knob, she almost yelped like a baby. She pulled the door towards her and opened the door.

The smile on her face disappeared and was replaced by a look of confusion. She took a quick look back into her rooms and back at her new surroundings, and the contrast was staggeringly obvious.

She wasn't in a hospital. Instead, someone had gone a great mile for her to assume that she was in one. The room she had thought was a VIP room was just a standard room in a normal-looking house.

How did she get here? What was she doing in a strange apartment? Had she been kidnapped? Her heartbeat increased exponentially. This wasn't the time to think of this. Instead, she should be looking for a way to get out of here.

Her face lit up when she realized that she was close to the front door. She hurried as fast as her legs could carry her and headed for the door while still leaning against the pole for support. As she reached for the door, she saw a shadow on the front door and immediately hid in the small store near the door.

She knew the shadow might not be a bad person, but she wasn't about to take chances. The new person opened the door and entered the house, and she held her breath.

She leaned gently and saw the feet of a person. He was a man. Her teeth clattered, and she quickly put her arms over her mouth before he heard her, but it was futile because he suddenly stopped.

A sound of fear almost escaped her lips, but she quickly covered her mouth and continued to hold her breath. She eyed the front door and calculated if she could outrun him to the door. She shook her head, dismissing the idea. Even if she wasn't feeling sick, she wasn't an athlete or a fast runner.

"Hello?" The man said.

The woman bites her bottom lips together. He has tracked her down! In dismay, she thought, is this how she would die, with no one knowing where she was? "She is still sleeping, yes. I think she still thinks she is at a hospital. I know what I am supposed to do. Yes, I will do it right now," the man said. He ended the call.

The woman sighed in relief when she found out he hadn't her, but he was just making a call, but she knew that her triumph was short-lived. She knew he would find out that she had run away soon enough.

As soon as she noticed him heading for her room, she dashed out of the store as fast as her jelly legs could carry her and ran towards the door, opening it and running outside. She heard a low "oh" behind her as the man ran towards her, but she was free!

Wait a minute?

"Dad?" her heart elated as she rushed towards the man, standing outside the house with some other men.

"Felicia?" Felix cried as his daughter literally jumped into his embrace. He tightened his arm around his daughter as if he was never going to let her go.

"Dad...dad," Felicia checked, tapping his arm for air.

Felix pulled back, gently but not completely. He looked at her face as his own was washed with tears.

"Dad, why are you crying? What happened?" She paused as if she remembered something. "Wait, I was in an accident, right?"

Felix smiled and nodded. "Yes, you were, darling, but you are safe now."

"I don't understand. How in God's name did I survive that? Am I dead right now? Is this some kind of limbo before I go to heaven or something?" Felicia asked. She wasn't stupid, but many things didn't make sense, turning around gently, she saw the man in the house earlier coming towards her. She nestled deeper into her father's protective arm.

The reflection of the sun covered his face as he walked towards her, but there was still something about the way he carried himself that made her catch her breath. There was a dark intensity about him, as though the whole air around him was calling to his masculinity.

"Ms. Smith," the man greeted when he reached her front. "You shouldn't have run earlier."

Her first thought was that he must have stepped out of a painting. His smile seemed disarming, but something about him still made her feel unsettled, and her father's arm still felt like the safer place to be.

The painters in Shakespeare's time would have loved him, Felicia thought. There was something calm, exciting, and edgy around him. Lean and broad-shouldered, the man was the only thing she could see.

She realized she was holding her breath, waiting for him to grab her and pull her back into the house, even though her father's arm was wrapped against her small frame. Thankfully he didn't act like her over-imaginative brain. Instead, he just stood in front of her, smiling, but Felicia realized the smile wasn't reaching his eyes.

"Felicia meets Lloyd Dean," Felix said.

Felicia was still confused. Her father just mentioned the man's name as if it was supposed to answer all her questions.

"Dad, where I'm I? I don't care about any Lloyd. I want to go home," she said. "I want to speak with mum and Fran."

Felix bit his bottom lips gently. "Let's go back into the house, and I. Will explains everything."

"No!" Startled, she looks a hasty step out of the comfort of his arm. "Tell me what is going on now!"

"I will do that inside the house," Felix replied, a matter of fact. He smiled, amused when he saw Felicia frown, still standing her ground.

"What is funny, dad?" Felicia retreated another step after seeing the mischievous grin on his face. "What are you doing?"

Felicia didn't have much time to gather her thoughts because she was swept high in the sky in her father's arm. She heard a light chuckle and knew it was from Mr. Shakespeare behind her.

"Dad, put me down!"

"Once we are back in the house, I will do that," he promised, and true to his word, as soon as the door closed behind him, he put her gently on a sofa in the living room.

Francis glared at her father, but she settled into the coach. She was tired and still very much weak. She wasn't treated in fighting with anyone. She just wanted to understand what was going on.

"So..." she nodded gently. "Explain"

Felix settled on the table in front of his daughter, patted her hair gently, and smiled. Felicia was surprised at her father's show of vulnerability, but she didn't say anything or pull away.

"What did you remember? What is the last thing you remember?" He asked her gently, holding her hands together in his large hands.

"I... em..." she paused and suddenly looked at him, as she remembered, "I was in an accident, my brake stopped working!"

Felix smiled. "What else? What do you remember after that?"

Felicia didn't know what to say. She looked from Mr. Shakespeare, who was leaning against a wall away from them but watching them attentively and back at her father.

"I'm I supposed to know something else?" Felicia asked, cracking her head, trying to remember if she had forgotten any details. "How I'm I still standing?"

"Because someone saved you after you fell into the water, "Felix pointed at Lloyd. "He is Officer Lloyd Dean, he was assigned to you, so when you had the accident, he saved you fell off the bridge."

Felicia looked at Lloyd again. He definitely had the look of someone who could go into combat mode and save someone from falling off the bridge.

"Thanks for saving me," Felicia thanked him, bowing slightly in his direction.

Lloyd nodded in her direction but didn't say a word.

"So, where I'm I?" Felicia asked, looking around her surroundings. "I did get hurt, so why didn't you take me to the hospital, where I'm I?"

"New York"

"And I... " Felicia earshot up. Her head hadn't processed what Felix had said earlier. "What do you mean, New York?"

"We flew you to New York after the incident. We knew that you were in more danger, and we had to make sure that you were safe."

"I thought I was going to Florida," Felicia mused, "and you keep saying we, where is mum? Didn't she follow you?"

Felix's bottom lips wobbled for a second, Felicia thought, but she could be wrong, nothing ever scares her father, but she was confident that she saw the look that passed between her father and Lloyd.

"What happened again?" Felicia sighed, frustration seeping into her voice.

"I meant I and the police made the decision to bring you to New York instead of Florida, and your mother doesn't know about this "

"Wait" Felicia raised her hand. "What do you mean mum doesn't know?"

Felix shared firmly with his daughter. "Everyone thinks you are dead."

Felicia blinked hard as her brain scrambled to comprehend what she had just heard. "I don't understand."

Lloyd finally moved from the wall and dropped a newspaper on the table in front of Felicia. Felicia licked her lips suddenly. Her throat felt dry.

In big letters on the front page of *The sun*, the news wrote **Ms. Felicia Smith was laid to rest today, the 25th of April, 2021...**Felicia glanced at the two men in front of her for answers, but none were forthcoming.

"What do you mean by this" she picked up the paper. The picture at the bottom of the headline caught her eyes. She saw her parents and Charles in front of a closed casket dressed in black. "You had a burial, but mum thinks I am dead?" Tears filled Felicia's eyes as she stared at her picture, her heartbreaking. "What about Fran? Why..."

"Hmm-" Felix bites his bottom lips again.

"I don't understand. What happened?"

"She fainted and couldn't attend the burial," Felix finally answered.

"Wait, let me get this straight. My mum and sister think I am dead. My sister likely fainted on finding out that I am dead, but she couldn't attend my fake burial and is likely beating herself up. Did I miss anything, or is there more?" She asked coldly.

"Yes, that sums it up" Felix held her hands tightly in his. "Do you know how scared I was when I thought that I would lose you? If your mother and sister's heart would break, I can live with that-"

"But-"

"Let me finish. The police suspected that the entire family had been bugged, which is why the crazy man was likely aware of all of our movements. So we decided it would be best if everyone, including yourself, assumed you were relocating to Florida rather than New York."

"You didn't bank on my breaks getting cut," Felicia said.

"We didn't," Felix said, a matter of fact.

"I-" Felicia's body shook as she remembered the accident. " I almost died!"

"We had plans of our own too. The police thought faking your death was the best thing," Felix said quickly. "The car was fine. We will stop you before the airport. We had it all figured out, the extra body, the explosion, but we didn't think he would also cut the brakes. We found video footage after the accident of someone cutting the brakes, but the footage isn't clear, and the culprit hasn't been found."

"But-"

Felix stops up frustrated, throwing his hands in the air. "You think I wanted to go this far? I had to pull all stones unturned to make sure you were safe. I couldn't tell you beforehand that we were going to plan your death in case the news leaked" he ran his hand over his eyes. "I am tired. I can't remember the last time I slept. The accident was supposed to be fake and not real."

And that was when it struck Felicia that her father was also going through hell and not just her.

"So, what next now?" Felicia asked, resigned.

Felix sighed in relief and sat back quickly in front of Felicia. "Lloyd is here to protect you. You are friends sharing accommodation together."

"Me and ...him" Felicia pointed at the hunk who stood silently away from them.

"Yes," Felix added, enthusiast. "You need to listen to him. You are in his protective care." He laughed at an inside joke. "The police actually thought of making both of you married couples, but I told them that you would freak out."

Felicia chuckled nervously. "Yeah, right. I would freak out," she said, trying to tear her gaze from the masterpiece that was his body.

"I need to leave now," Felix said, standing up to his feet. "I only came here because it would be better to hear the whole situation from me and not a stranger."

Felicia started standing, but Felix stopped her.

"I can find my way out," he said gently as he touched her face. "Also, Felicia-"

"Yes?"

"You can't call your mum or sister " he saw her heart drop when he said those words. "It is dangerous for all of you. If the line is bugged, that psychopath can find out where you are or find out that you are Alice and hurt Chloe or Felicia so that they can get the truth."

Felicia nodded and watched as her father walked over to the door. Felix stopped when he got to the door and brought his phone out of his pocket. The look on his face told Felicia that it was likely either her mother or Fran.

She stood up and dragged the IV pole, walking towards Felix, still staring at his ringing phone warily. Her eyes caught sight of the Caller ID. It was Fran.

"I will talk to her later" Felix started putting the phone back into his pocket.

Felicia held his hand. "No, please talk to her. I won't say anything. I just want to hear her voice."

Felix nodded slightly, used his finger to slide to the right to answer the call, and brought it to his ear.

"Hello" Fran's warm voice came clearly over the line.

"Hello, darling " Felix turned so that he was facing Felicia.

"When are you coming back?" There was a smile in her voice. "I want you to come back before the seventh "

"I will be there. " Felix said, lightly touching Felicia's nose. "I will always be there for you, daughter."

Fran laughed. "Uh-uh, I know that dad, but I want you here because it was Felicia 's one-month anniversary, and I wanted all of us to be together."

"Okay" Felix saw Felicia flinch when she heard that she had been bedridden for almost a month. He was proud of the fact that she put a hand over her mouth to hide her surprise.

"Bye, dad."

"Bye, daughter. I love you."

"Hmm?" Fran chuckled. "You are a little too affectionate today. It must be the weather in Florida today."

"I love you," he repeated, pointedly at Felicia.

"I love you too, dad. Come home soon," Fran finally voiced out.

Felix placed the phone in his pocket after the call ended and squared his shoulders. There was a hesitation in the way he carried himself.

"So, this is it," Felix said, looking everywhere but his daughter. "I guess I am leaving now. I will contact you through Lloyd, so listen to everything he says."

Felicia nodded without speaking. She just stared at her father's face as he tried to act nonchalant. There were new lines across his face that she hadn't noticed the last time she spoke to her. She realized that he looked ten years older, and it was because he was trying to keep herself.

Felicia couldn't help herself. She tiptoed and planted a light kiss on his cheek. "I love you too, dad," Felicia said softly. "Now, leave before I hold you and say that you can't go."

"I-"

"Don't turn around. I will do everything Lloyd says, and I promise to stay safe. So don't worry about me and go back to London. " Felicia noticed that he was turning around. "Don't look back, go, dad."

She pushed him out of the door and closed it, shut it behind him. She leaned against the closed door and put a fist in her mouth to stop the sound of her sobs.

Her body slid down to the floor, where she sat and poured out her heart. The tears fell as if she had a reserve tank of water stored in her eyes. The fact that a stranger she never knew could cause any harm, could inflict this amount of pain on her family was unforgivable.

Then and there, she made a promise to make sure that that psychopath's dream never came true. She would never ever fall in love or get married, and no job would ever win!

She noticed her father's handkerchief on the table he had sat on earlier, and a fresh round of sob shook her body.

CHAPTER FOUR

Lloyd Dean was used to 'protecting' a lot of spoilt brats because their parents had more money than sense and needed someone to babysit their brats for the time being.

Tired of doing jobs like this. Lloyd had literally begged the Chief Officer that he would rather have desk duty than see another brat, and Daniel Ford had agreed.

"I promise Lloyd, this is the last one," Daniel had said. "You know the situation with this Wedding psychopath. So, help this time, and after this, I won't let you take any job you hate."

After Daniel also promised to move Lloyd to the Violent crime unit, he had readily agreed, and for a month, he had been on guard duty. Following Felicia everywhere while staying out of sight. He had found every early that she was different from anyone he had ever met.

There was something about how she selflessly tried to help everyone around her even while inconveniencing herself, but she hadn't seemed to care.

His job was to make sure nothing happened to the rich man's daughter, but under his watch, Felicia had almost died. Daniel might have praised him for saving Felicia's life at the last second, but Lloyd still felt guilty. Despite the 'save' that everyone seemed hell-bent on praising him for. Felicia had still sustained injuries that left her bedridden for almost a month.

Now, staring at her delicate features sitting at the bottom of the door with a look of loss. Lloyd had his urge to hold her tight against his chest and promise her that he would never let her get hurt by anything ever again. He also wished he knew who the Wedding psychopath was to rain fell fire on the creep for making her hurt this much.

Felicia was still under medication. She shouldn't be crying this much. he thought. He walked over to where she sat with her face buried between her knees. He tried to tap her but stopped himself. He might have cared for her for the last month, but he was still a stranger to her.

So, he slid beside her and just sat there silently and watched her pour her heart out. He reached for her again but stopped himself once again, but Felicia raised her head and stared at him.

"I need-" she searched around but didn't find what she was looking for. Then she reached for the bottom of Lloyd's oversized shirt. Lloyd blinked in surprise as Felicia brought the sweater to her face.

"Wait, what?" Lloyd stretched his hand to stop her, but it was too late. Felicia brought the shirt to her nose and blew her nose into it. Not one, not twice but three times!

Then she stared back at him with tear swollen eyes. "I think I messed up your shirt."

Lloyd raised his brow. "You think?"

"I am sorry" Felicia covered her face and suddenly started crying all over again.

What just happened? Startled, Lloyd glanced at Felicia anew. The girl was the one who used his cloth as tissue, and now she was crying as if she was the victim? Maybe he had overpraised her before.

All rich brats are the same!

A lightweight on his shoulder brought him back to reality. He relaxed his fist and stared at Felicia's sleeping head on his shoulder. At that moment, he forgot about her crazy stunt some minute ago and stared at her.

Lloyd realized that he could just look at her all day. Her feature was more relaxed when she was asleep than when she was awake when she looked like she was about to shoulder the responsibilities of the world on her dainty shoulders. He wished he could take all her troubles and solve every one of them. He raised his hand to touch her long lashes but quickly slapped his arm away with his other reasonable hand.

Something about Felicia Smith would be his end because he lost all reasonable functions anytime he was around the woman. He is just meant to act like her roommate for the time being. Till the Wedding, Psychopath is caught, and after that, Felicia would leave this house and go back to her perfect life, and he would return to the police force.

Girls like Felicia don't mingle with guys like him, so he better focus on his job. Protect and deliver the 'parcel' to safety and not overthink the job.

Daniel would say. "Thinking kills a man while in his job. So don't ever use your brain, Lloyd. It brings more harm than good"

***

The reflection of the sun against her face woke Felicia up. She yawned, stretched, and turned around to see herself looking into the most beautiful face she had ever seen up close.

Instinctively, she licked her bottom lips, and her mouth suddenly felt dry. Lloyd's head was rested against the door with his eyes closed. His chiseled face and rugged jawline looked like something the sculptor spent some extra time on. His nose was long and pointed, and her hand itched to touch it. Most men always had thick brows, and he was no different, but his long lashes caught her attention.

Felicia couldn't help herself. She placed a finger over his closed eyes to measure his eyelashes, then she almost gasped out loud when she realized that his lashes were longer than hers.

"It is long," she whispered, mesmerized by his lashes. "How can a man be this beautiful?"

"I'm I that beautiful?"

Startled, Felicia jumped back from him, but he grabbed the hand on his face without opening his eyes. He placed her palm on his cheek gently.

"I am human and not some toy, ma'am," he said.

Felicia snatched her hand and backed away from him quickly.

"And when did I say that you weren't?" She sounded pissed as she stared at the self-righteous man.

"You were staring at me as if I wasn't " Lloyd shrugged nonchalantly as he hot to his feet. "If that wasn't your intention, then I am sorry. I just didn't appreciate it when anyone stared at me the way you did".

Felicia scoff. She couldn't believe what she was hearing. One thing to always expect from men is audacity. Who did he think he was? Chris Evan's?

"Don't worry, I won't be anywhere near you for that to happen again, sir," Felicia promised. "You are, sir, right?"

Lloyd groaned while running his hand through his thick black hair. "I am sorry."

"Huh?" Felicia was taken aback. "I don't understand."

"When I wake up in the morning. I am grumpy, and I tend to lash out" Lloyd smiled. "I didn't mean to raise my voice at you. Our first meeting wasn't supposed to go like this"

Felicia looked at him for a second too long, then she shrugged and decided to forgive him. This was the man she would be staying with. She can be as close as possible to him the best thing she can do.

"Apology accepted, " Felicia said simply.

A low growl.

"That wasn't me!" Felicia waved her hands frantically, but the low growl came from her stomach again. That second, she wished the floor looked just open and swallowed her, but nothing like that happened.

"I can see that it wasn't you" Lloyd chuckled at her cuteness. "Why don't we do this, you get changed, and I get changed. Let's go out and get something to eat."

"We can go out?" Felicia asked, surprised.

"Yes, we can" He smiled. "Just a few rules. One, no pictures of any kind. Two, no social media presence whatsoever. Three, at no point in time can you call your family without telling"

"So, I am a prisoner. Got it!" Felicia gave a feral grin. "So, where are my stuff? Or don't I have any?"

Lloyd stared at Felicia intensively. The anger on her face was clear as day. He had noticed from following her around that she wasn't someone who knew how to hide her feeling, but there was another emotion on her face too, but he couldn't figure it out.

"Upstairs, the first room on the right is yours," Lloyd explained. "Your dad brought your stuff from London."

Felicia nodded curtly and headed up the stairs. Lloyd waited a few seconds before climbing the stairs towards his room. He also needed to freshen up and change his cloth.

While washing his body under the shower, Lloyd suddenly remembered that he hadn't taken his sleeping pills last night, and he had slept like a log for more than twelve hours. That had not happened in months. He had had to take medications to sleep for a long time, and even when he did, sometimes he either woke up screaming from his nightmares, or the pills didn't work at all.

So, what was different about yesterday night that made him feel light and excited for the start of a new day?

***

Felicia settled for a tanked top, high waist jeans, and booth. She stepped out of the house to find Lloyd already in a Honda accord sports car waiting for her. She took her time walking from the front porch, the lawn, and then towards the vehicle. She still felt weak and hadn't really eaten anything yesterday.

"Miss" Lloyd stepped out of the car and helped her open the door to the passenger's seat.

"Thanks," she said as she slid into the seat.

Lloyd is such a gentleman, she thought.

He slid back into the passenger seat and tapped his hand on the steering as if he was thinking.

"So, where should we go?" He turned to ask her.

"Wait, you want my opinion?" Felicia laughed richly. "I don't even know where I am. I know we are in New York alright, but I don't know where."

Lloyd had to laugh too. He hadn't thought of that. "We are in Battery Park City, it is in lower Manhattan, and I think it is a relatively calm neighborhood. Everyone minded her own business.

Felicia raised a brow. "I still have no idea where we can go, and I am famished already."

"let's go to Soho, it is about ten minutes, and after eating, we can go sightseeing.

"Really? Can we do that?" Felicia held his hand and bounced on the chair excitedly. "I was scared that I would have to stay cooped up inside the house."

"You are that happy?"

"Yes, excited is more like it" she glanced down at her hands and realized that she was holding his hand in her quickly. She let go of his hands and chuckled nervously.

A dangerous smile played at the side of his lips, he leaned close to her, and she sank back into the car door hastily. A sharp whiff of rose flower filled his senses as he came close to her. Lloyd suddenly noticed that his lips were an inch away from hers. He inhaled sharply.

"Wh-what do you want?" she stuttered. Her voice broke as she backed away from Lloyd, but there was no place to run to.

"This" He closed his eyes to block her out of his senses, then raised his hand over her shoulder to pull the seat belt. His index finger lightly brushed her skin as he helped her lock the belt in place. He wasn't sure if he heard or imagined the gasp from her, but he definitely felt the shock that seeped from that slight touch to his whole body.

He pulled back quickly." I am just trying to fix your seat belt. What were you thinking," he asked, amused?

"Nothing," she added a little too quickly. She turned her face to gaze out the window, feeling stupid as she mentality smacked herself on the head when she saw the mischievous smile on his face.

"I never take one step unless everyone is strapped in" He explained his behavior as he started the car, but he only meant something else. He wouldn't kiss or touch her without her permission.

"Of course," Felicia felt obliged to say. Embarrassed, she stared in every direction but Lloyd's. Instead, she feasted her eyes on the sight outside the car.

The car drove past parks filled with lush greenery vibrant yet calm colors. It was New York, but no one seemed to be in any hurry to get anywhere. There were loads of people, jogging, children playing and cycling peacefully on the side of the road.

People laid on the floor, some with families chatting away, while others napped in to soak in the spring's vitamin D. Watching all of them made her smile somewhat that she forgot about her earlier embarrassment with Lloyd.

She suddenly caught sight of a food truck under a tree, and not too far, some people were relishing the food on some outdoor seating.

"Let's eat that, "she pointed in excitement.

"No," He refused bluntly.

Felicia turned around to face him sharply. "But you said-

"I said I wanted to get you real food," he stressed the word 'real' unapologetically. "You didn't eat anything yesterday, and you need something trustworthy in your system this morning and not junk food."

Felicia rolled her eyes and slumped deeper into the chair. "And how do you know it's junk?"

"Because I have a brain?

"Well. Wait, wait?" she shot out of the chair to glare at Lloyd.

"If you like, continue glaring at me. You can burrow holes into my face. We are eating healthy until you are off medications," his voice low and resonant. He raised a packet of meds to her face. Felicia wanted to argue, but the voice of the man-made her think otherwise.

Something about him showed her that he didn't have to raise his voice to get his point across. He was like her father in any way. She had been trying not to think about her father all day, but Lloyd's attentions reminded her of him in so many ways.

Felicia shook her head. No, she wasn't going to cry. She thought. Instead, she closed her eyes and tried to fall asleep. Yes, that would be better than thinking of sad memories.

***

Felicia woke up with a start, turned to her side, and noticed that Lloyd had also fallen asleep and the car was packed. Some men exude sexuality, intentionally or not, and send you into overdrive whether they want to or they don't. An excellent example of such a man is Lloyd.

He would easily get into the industry if he ever chose to be a model. His lush, thick dark hair and the subtle air around him say that he didn't know how he looked or cared about it.

The pointed yet broad nose complemented his prominent cheekbones. Handsome in an understated way, his jaw and warrior-like shoulders spoke of strength. She could imagine his big arm around her tiny waist crushing her against his hard…

Stop it! Felicia chided herself quickly when she realized her train of thought. She quickly found something else to distract her from the hunk beside her. He glanced out the window and saw Soho in all of its beauty.

Once, she heard a saying that New York neighborhoods were hard to define, but Soho was definitely different. First of all, it was busy and beautiful. She had heard and seen pictures of the famous cast-iron buildings but seeing them from this distance gave her chills. The roadside screens filled everywhere, advertising everything possible.

Its messy grid of streets and narrow alleyways was buzzing, grubby, swanky, and sexy in equal parts. It called to Felicia's senses to explore.

"Wow," she exclaimed out loud.

"You are awake."

"Yes," Felicia turned around and smiled excitedly like a baby. "I didn't want to wake you.

"I wasn't asleep. I just closed my eyes to think. I didn't want to wake you up yet."

"Thanks" Felicia realized that she was actually thankful to him. "I really needed the nap even though I slept all night."

"I need to pack. I got us a reservation at *Quo Vadis.* I think you will love it," He explained to her gently. "But I could be wrong."

"Okay," Felicia answered.

The ride to the car park was short but worth it. Felicia had a chance to stretch her long legs that felt cramped inside the car.

They walked their path down the less busy street.

A young man in his early twenties was riding a bicycle towards them. As he got close to them, Lloyd tugged Felicia's arm, clasping his tightly around her smaller one, pulling her to the other side of the road.

'Watch it, Felicia," Lloyd cried.

Felicia was too shocked that she didn't have time to react. She just found herself falling back against him as she narrowly avoided the cyclist, splashing puddle water on her.

She blinked rapidly. Everything happened so fast - one minute, she was thinking of what she ordered, and the next minute, she was pressed tightly against Lloyd's chest. Her heart was beating unnaturally fast and loud.

"Did you get hurt?" he asked, his voice filled with concern. He held Felicia tightly against him with one arm and used the other arm to look her over. "Are you sure you have no injuries?"

Lloyd nodded. That was the only sensible answer her brain could give. She inhaled the scent of his body wash, coupled with his aftershave. It was exhilarating. She inhaled deeply.

She tried to look away, but she couldn't tear her gaze away from his lips. She swallowed hard and unconsciously raised her hand to his face to tuck a strand of hair that had fallen to the side of his face. Lloyd's eyes darkened under her touch, and he tightened his arm around her.

Felicia continued her exploration. At least that was all she meant to do, but her thumb ended up trailing his cheek and brushing his lower lips.

"How is it so soft?" Felicia asked, glancing up at him. A jolt of realization suddenly hit her. One minute, she was in his arms, and the next, she was jumping out of his arms like a scared cat.

"I didn't mean to that; I was taken away- I mean…oh God! Why am I blabbering like a fool" Felicia wished the floor would open up and swallowed her for the second time that day.

Lloyd's lips quirked up in a half-smile as he watched Felicia try to explain herself.

"I am fine, Felicia. You don't need to be bothered about it. It happens," he said softly.

Oh... he must meet a lot of women. He can't be offended because someone as plain as her touched his face, or can he? Felicia mused as she turned around and continued walking up the path. She stepped forward, trying to distance between them because she needed the space.

A hand, hot against her skin, held hers. Felicia turned slightly to see Lloyd beside her, holding her hand.

"We- we don't -

"I know, let's just walk like this. You look tired, and I haven't fulfilled my promise of feeding you yet."

"Yeah, right," Felicia answered much too quickly. She didn't want to admit it, but she loved the feel of his hand against hers. It was burning, but at the same time, it was comforting, and she felt protected with that simple touch.

***

QUA VODIS was nestled in 26 East 63rd Street near the corner of Madison Avenue. The place breathes history even from a distance. Its impressive architectural design was first established in 1946 by two Italians. Lloyd and Felicia were given a window seat which was insisted by Lloyd. Felicia knew the reasons for his action but shook her head to dismiss the thought,

The only thing she wanted to think about was the food. Lloyd ordered smoked eel sarnie and a pie. In contrast, Felicia ordered a crab and fennel salad coated in a fresh vinaigrette and came with generous helpings of crab meat. Felicia wished she had her phone to take a picture of the artistic masterpiece on her plate, but she didn't have a phone, and he didn't want to ask Lloyd for his.

He had this official 'don't mess with me look,' so she sighed intensely, picked up her cutleries, and started devouring the sumptuous appetizer in front of her. Felicia groaned as the first spoon touched her lips.

"Is it that good?"

Felicia opened her eyes to find Lloyd staring at her with a hooded expression. Then something dark and alluring about the way he cocked his head to one side to just look at her.

"This is delicious!" Felicia affirmed, dismissing the look on Lloyd's face. She was sure she imagined it. Instead, she focused on finishing the food. Within a few minutes, Felicia cleared her plate. The spoon in her mouth as she stared at Lloyd's almost untouched plate.

"Are you not going to eat that?" Felicia couldn't help asking.

Lloyd laughed. "You always surprised me, Ms. Smith."

"Why," she shrugged. "Because I asked if you are going to eat your food?"

"Not really," he shook his head, still smiling "...and no, I am not eating this anymore. I suddenly feel hungry for something else."

Felicia was sure that she didn't imagine the look in Lloyd's eyes this time. His eyes were tearing at hers with wanting, and the tension between them was so thick she could feel it against her skin.

She grabbed the glass of water close to her, downed the whole drink into her mouth, and gasped in pain when it burned her throat. He glanced from her hand to the table to realize that she had taken Lloyd's glass and not hers.

"What have you done?" His excellent gentle hands collected the glass from her.

"Ah...um" Felicia tried to make sense of what had happened. Her eyes suddenly felt heavy. "I ordered water, and I drank water, but it wasn't water. It was your whiskey!"

"How do you feel?"

"Are you asking if I am drunk because I am not" she stood up to show that she was fine but slumped back on the chair as her legs gave way under her? "See, I am perfectly fine."

"I can see that," Lloyd said, raising his hand to call the waiter. At the same time, he stood up to sit beside Felicia before doing something as stupid as running out of the restaurant.

The waiter came around with the bill. Lloyd quickly paid and started leading Felicia out of the restaurant. He was thankful that she didn't act up in the restaurant, but she refused to follow him as soon as they stepped outside.

"I am not going anywhere with you" Felicia folded her arm across her chest and frowned stubbornly. "If you don't do what I want, then I am not going anywhere!"

"I will do anything you want. Let's just go, " Lloyd pleaded, pulling her towards him, but she stood her ground firmly for someone bedridden a few days ago.

"You haven't done what I wanted yet!" Felicia stamped her foot like a baby.

Lloyd threw his hand in the air. "Fine. I will do it. Now let's go!"

Felicia smiled sheepishly. "If that is true, then kiss me."

"Huh?"

Felicia brought her face towards Lloyd, her lips puckered with her eyes closed. "I said kiss me."

Lloyd staggered backward away from Felicia. "You are crazy and drunk. I am getting you back home."

"I guess you won't do what I want" Felicia opened her eyes and pulled away from him.

"No, so let's go."

He reached for her hand, but she pulled it away and smiled mischievously. She took a small step backward away from Lloyd and another.

"Stop moving and come back here!" He growls.

"You will have to catch me first" she turned around and ran down the street.

"I caught you."

Lloyd caught her in a few seconds. She was no match for him. Lloyd thought, even if she wasn't a woman, he was a police officer, and he had trained for stuff like this.

He was wrong. It happened so fast in a blink of an eye that Lloyd realized he was no longer the capture but the prisoner. Felicia locked her hands around him and glued her body to him.

"Will you kiss me or not" her eyes dancing in the morning sun like that of a gypsy.

"No," Lloyd shook his head firmly, waving his finger at her as if he was talking to a baby. "I would love it. If you stop now. "

Felicia suddenly unlocked her hand from his back and pulled away. "I am sorry, I understand," she said between hiccups.

"Thank God," he heaved a sigh of relief, throwing his hand in her air to show that he was free.

"Can we leave now" Felicia continued hiccupping "we don't want people to see you with an ugly woman like me."

Felicia walked hurried in front, but Lloyd caught up with her and turned her around to face him.

"What do you mean by ugly?" He growled, his eyes darling with each word. "You mean you?"

"Yes, if I was beautiful, you would have kissed me, but you didn't believe I am ug-"

Before she could finish the last word, he suddenly pushed her against the wall but with his hand on the back of her head. He tilted her head so that she was looking into his eyes.

"What-"

"Remember, you asked for this," he added darkly before his lips firmly covered hers in a kiss that made Felicia lose whatever remained of her senses.

***

All Lloyd had meant to do was to shut Felicia up. He couldn't believe the blasphemy he had heard from her lips. How could she call this body that fitted perfectly against his ugly? So, he had kissed her to shut her up and give her what she wanted.

But her soft, naive lips drew him more profound. He was thirsty and hungry despite her body against his. He wanted more, so he kissed her bottom lips and then the top of her lips. Felicia gasps against his arm, and that gives his tongue the invitation it has been looking for.

He punches into the depth of her mouth. She wiggled, and her body pulsated against him as she arched for more. He could feel her hands in his hair as she pulled her closer. He liked that. Everything she was doing was making his senses shut down.

The way she controlled him, pulled away, lured him back, all at the right moment. He heard her breathing heavily against him, and he felt his legs go weak under him simultaneously, but he didn't stop. His whole body tingled with desire, and he wrapped his arm more tightly against her so that she could feel what she was doing to him.

He claimed her mouth again, hungry and intense, his hand slipped under her top and cupped one ripe bud, and he felt her melt in his arms, her eyes closed as she groaned in pleasure.

She was the most beautiful thing he had ever seen. It was as if time had stopped, and they didn't care about the world. Nobody mattered or existed. All he cared about was...

What was he doing? He pulled away from Felicia swiftly, putting enough distance between them. The first thing he did was to look around his surroundings. He signed in relief when he realized he was at the end of the street, so they weren't actually giving curious passersby a show.

A wave of guilt came over him when he saw his reflection in a glass of a closed flower shop. He looked like a predator, he was red, messy and the bulge between his legs was as clear as day. He risked one looked at Felicia and saw her staring at him intensively without saying a word.

He was supposed to protect her and not try to weave his way into her underpants.

"We should get to the car" Lloyd couldn't believe that was his voice. He sounded hoarse and throaty.

"Why did you stop," Felicia asked, leaning against the wall non-committal.

"You will be the death of me" Lloyd threw his hands in the hair, pacing around a circle. "You are still drunk. Let's just go."

"Unless you tell me why you stopped, then I am not taking a single step away from here" she shrugged like she had all the time in the world.

Lloyd couldn't believe his ears. Had there been a body switch that he didn't know about? The Felicia he followed around London was timid, shy, and easygoing but this woman standing in front of him was anything but that.

"Can we leave this road and talk elsewhere?" He asked gently.

"Nope," she shook her head, still maintaining her ground. "What I asked for, or I don't move."

"You know that I can easily carry you?"

"But I don't think that you want to," she chuckled wickedly. "-

touch me."

Lloyd glared at her but suddenly smiled as if he wasn't frowning a minute ago. He scoffed. Then he strolled gently towards her and held her hands in his.

"See, I have no problem coming close to you."

"But you ran-"

"You have a wide imagination, baby girl," he sighed. "I am too tired to drive. Let's chill somewhere and go back later."

Lloyd started walking with Felicia in tow but realized soon that she was too tired to walk. He groaned in frustration because it looked like the universe was coming together to conspire against him. He walked in front of her and squatted to the ground.

"Climb"

"You want to piggyback me?" She asked curiously.

"Well, I am not trying to fly with you now, genius," his voice laced with sarcasm.

Felicia didn't seem to care about his tone. She lowered herself to his back and wrapped her arms around his neck. Lloyd regretted the decision as soon as he implemented it.

Her whole body was pressed against his once more. He closed his eyes, breathing heavily.

The heavens were definitely conspiring against him. He thought as he carried his bundle of guilty pleasure to the car.

CHAPTER FIVE

The hotel clerk was clearly amused when Lloyd walked in with Felicia on his back. He didn't try to hide it. Actually, everyone in the lobby was watching both of them. Everyone could see that she wasn't dead but sleeping from the way she kept turning on his back.

Earlier, when he had gotten back to the car, he realized that the car was overheating and refused to start. He had caused his luck once again.

"Please!" He had hit the steering wheel in anger as he sent a prayer and plea to the heavens to stop testing and throwing troubles his way. Since he had no other choice, he had locked the car, called the insurance company, and headed to this hotel.

"Can I have the keys?" Lloyd asked again.

"Oh, sorry, sir" the young clerk stopped staring at Lloyd and Felicia and handed him the key.

"Thanks," he thanked the clerk through clenched teeth and headed for the elevator.

"Kiss me, officer," Came a sultry voice behind him.

Lloyd stopped in his tracks when he heard Felicia's voice ringing through the lobby. He groaned inwardly. Lloyd adjusted her on his back and realized that she was still sleeping. He also turned and noticed people staring at them.

This is not good. Lloyd pondered quickly. Felicia should avoid attracting undue attention to herself. Fortunately, no one was flashing a camera in their face to record them. Lloyd punched the bottom of the elevator and hurried inside before Felicia did anything cuter.

Cute? How could he think of this troublesome bundle as cute? What amazed him was that everything she's done since morning made her endeared to him. He mentally smacked his head, shaking it to dismiss his thoughts. He has to stop thinking about the way Felicia felt perfectly against him when he kissed her earlier or the way she moaned against his lips.

Jeez...he groaned again. He was still thinking about Felicia.

The elevation came to a stop, and he walked over to their room on shaky legs. He opened the door and entered the room. Earlier, he had wanted to get separate rooms for them. Because he hadn't made a reservation earlier, most of the rooms were booked, and the only room available was this one.

Fortunately, it has two separate rooms, he reminded himself. He walked gently to the bed on the right side of the room, laid Felicia on the bed, and stepped back to stare at her. The bed creaked softly as she turned in her sleep so that her face was inches away from his. Lloyd swallowed hard, falling on his ass and hands. This tiny woman scared him, silly. The best thing he can do for himself is to stay away from her before he starts doing something as dangerous as falling for her.

He groaned as he picked himself up while walking over to the other side of the room where his bed was. He looked out the window and watched the afternoon bustle from the window. He was far up on the third floor of the hotel.

The ARLO hotel was perfection in a tiny package. The room was not as big as what he was used to, but it had everything you needed. Attention to detail is evident throughout. Felicia would love this place when she wakes up.

Stop it...don't think about her! What was wrong with him? He'd never been this distracted before while working. But he found his wind wandering every second towards the dark-headed woman in the opposite room.

What was that? He snapped out of his reverie. As quick as a flash, he was already in Felicia's room. He had heard her voice from his room, but he saw that she was still fast asleep when he got to her room. He took a quick look around the room to ensure no one else was in her room.

When he was confident that it was just Felicia talking in her sleep. He finally heaves a sigh of relief, rubbing his face with his palms. She looked peaceful, like an angel while she slept, and not like the stress she was putting her brain into. He heard her groan and noticed that she was slightly shivering.

Lloyd noticed a soft duvet on the end of the bed. He carefully pulled it over her body, stopping it slightly below her chin, and tucked it in on her side. He raised his head to leave, but Felicia held his hand suddenly.

Startled, he turned around but noticed that she was still sleeping. He tried to remove his hand, but she protested and held his hand tighter. He chuckled to himself and bent to sit cross-legged on the small rug beside the bed. He didn't try to force his hand again, although he was sure it wouldn't be so hard.

He told himself that he would sit for a few minutes, then leave when Felicia was fully asleep…just a few minutes.

***

A few hours later, Felicia awoke up to Lloyd's subtle snores coming from the end of the bed. Sitting up, she noticed that his dark hair was slightly rumbled, messy but he still looked dangerously handsome.

There was a sexy ruggedness around him. He was sitting on the floor with his head on the edge of the bed…holding her hand! Felicia's heart did a double somersault, and she felt her heart stop for a second too long. Lloyd was the sexiest man she had been nearby.

Her pulse raced, and she licked her dry lips as the room suddenly felt warmer. Her gaze drifted lower to Lloyd's chest. The first three buttons were opened to expose his chest's broad, tanned expanse. How can someone's neck look so tasty?

If she just runs her fingers over that chest slowly, all over that big…or if she just places her lips and presses kiss over his neck down to his chest. Felicia slapped her head.

"Stop gawking," she muttered under her breath.

But if only she could stop! Furious with herself, she buried her head in the pillow close to her and screamed into the pillow. Her head jerked back up when she heard him groan. She saw him turn where he sat. She could have sworn that he looked uncomfortable.

If she helped him to the bed, he would be more comfortable. His back and legs must be hurting from the way he was sitting. Felicia mused as she stared at him in concern. She gently slipped out from under the duvet and out of bed.

Now the dilemma, how would she help him to the bed? Felicia smiled to herself. She knew Lloyd likely weighed twice her weight. Carrying his man to the bed was looking next to impossible.

Was it his big arm that was bigger than her thigh and hand combined or his whole muscular figure? Please drool and help him if you are going to! She chides herself. She fisted her palms as if to say, you can do this, girl.

Then she knelt beside him, but one of his arms over her neck, and tried to stand up, but her leg wobbled under her, and she met her ass on the floor. Undefeated, she put all her weight into her legs and smiled triumphantly when she saw him standing up.

Yes! Felicia finally helped him up and started helping him to the bed when a large hot hand came upon her waist. She looked up into Lloyd's sleepy- dreamy eyes.

"What are you doing?" he asked, his throaty baritone voice thick with sleep. The sound made her heart tense, and every reasonable sentence flew out of her head.

"Uh?"

"I said why…why are you?" his eyes were still full of sleep.

Felicia looked around the room for an answer. An idea occurred to her, so she held her free hand over his face, twirling her finger over his eyes.

"Dreaming, you are dreaming, Lloyd," she said softly, still moving her fingers. "Sleep, Go back to sleep. You are dreaming."

Lloyd closed his eyes. Felicia almost yelped in excitement but covered her mouth at the last minute. She settled into the bed and started stepping away when Lloyd wrapped his arms around her waist again, pulled her back, and turned her so that she was flat on her back and he was leaning over her.

"What I don't understand is why I would be dreaming about you?" Lloyd questioned. His eyes looked fully awake now.

'What?" Felicia's senses failed her for the second time within ten minutes.

"I am a hundred percent certain that you heard me," he said firmly, his voice dark and resonating.

Felicia glanced around the room and not into the dark blue eyes that looked like they could read everything in her soul and her heartbeat. She was sure he could hear it.

"I asked you a question, Felicia."

Felicia suddenly felt anger building within her. She didn't do anything wrong. There was no reason for her to be uneasy or intimidated around this man. So, she stared him straight in the face.

"I only wanted to help you, you were sitting on the floor, and it looked uncomfortable, and I thought it would be better if you slept on the bed," she added hurriedly. "I didn't mean anything by it."

Lloyd nodded gently. "Let's assume you didn't mean anything by this," he added, leaning closer to her right ear. "What about this morning? What did you mean by that?"

Felicia felt her breath caught in her throat. The way the air around her ear felt with his lips close by was doing strange things to her body. The sensitive part between her legs was tingling, making her cross her legs.

Also, could anyone tell her why her lips and mouth felt dry!

Still against her ear. "I think you are in the habit of not answering questions."

"I don't understand, "Felicia answered breathlessly. "I didn't do anything to you this morning."

Lloyd pulled back so that he was staring into her eyes. "Are you going to pretend right now?"

"But I-" Felicia stopped talking as she remembered a strange memory. She glanced at Lloyd's lips right above hers and quickly placed a hand over mouth, dismayed. "I didn't... did I? I did...I could have, "she stuttered in shock at herself.

"It seems you remembered," Lloyd glint mischievously as he stared down at Felicia.

Stunned, Felicia couldn't believe it. What her brain was telling her had to be a lie. She couldn't have been that bold, right? She couldn't have done all that. She couldn't have grabbed him like that...

"You know I had to back you," he said, staring at her discomfort but continuing anyway. "I piggybacked you from the lobby of this hotel to this room.

Shaking her head, she brushed a dainty finger in his face. "No, you didn't-"

"Should we ask the clerk tomorrow? How do you think you got in here?" He asked curiously. He trailed a finger into her hair, playing with a strand of her hair. "We are not in the restaurant anymore!"

For the first time, Felicia looked, really looked around the room. There was no doubt in what Lloyd had just said. She had no recollection of how she got into this room. This was the best time to apologize for her untoward behavior and close the chapter. However, she took one look at the man lying above her while still putting some distance between them.

Closing her eyes for a moment to gather her courage, she opened them and smiled dangerously at him. "I was drunk before, and that's why I acted like that," she said, reaching up to place her hands behind his waist to lock her arms around him. "I am not drunk right now."

"W-what?"

She felt his big body shudder against hers as the distance between them disappeared. A very tiny voice of reason tried to tell Felicia that this wasn't how Felix and Chloe Smith sensible daughter acted. She was the one who didn't make stupid and uncalculated risks. That was her twin sister, Francisca's job.

Frowning, she shook the thought of her family out of her head and smiled at Lloyd. Tonight, she just wanted to feel something different from fear, pain, or helplessness, and letting this man make love go her seems like the right way to go about it.

"You keep staring at me like a ghost," Felicia smiled wickedly, biting her button lips. "Lloyd, can you make love to me?"

CHAPTER SIX

Lloyd felt like his head and body weren't his anymore because he wasn't in total control of anything they did. "Are you crazy?"

Smiling, she shook her head. "I am perfectly fine."

Closing his eyes for a second, he tried to stand up to put distance between them. "No, you aren't. You are crazy" he waved his finger in Felicia's face."

"No, I am not."

She locked her arms tighter around him, catching him by surprise so that he fell back against her. Lloyd realized too late that his lips had somehow landed on top of Felicia's soft lips. He groaned in frustration, tempted to kiss her, but he pulled back at the last minute.

"Why? Why are you doing this to me? I am a stranger. Someone who is just here to protect you," he said, trying to appeal to her common sense.

Felicia shrugged indifferently. "I know, and that's why you are perfect."

"What do you mean?" He asked, raising his brow in question.

"I am a stranger. You are a stranger. I want to have sex, and you obviously want to," she said, pointing at his lower body which has grown visibly bigger against her thigh. "We don't have to complicate things. We are adults. I know what I want, and so do you."

Lloyd didn't know why he felt hurt by her words. To be honest, Felicia was a stranger to him, and there was no reason for her words to hurt him on the tiniest bit, but there was something a little bitter on his throat. He cleared his throat with a slight cough and determination.

"I am not supposed to be fraternizing with my clients," he cautioned her, but the words were directed at him so that he should know his place. He pulled away from her again but with more determination this time. "I will go sleep in my room."

Felicia started saying something but shook her head instead. She watched Lloyd stand up from the bed and start walking out of the room.

"Goodnight," Lloyd said in a throaty voice, filled with emotion.

"Was it because I wasn't beautiful?" Felicia asked softly, her voice a little above a whisper. "Is that why you didn't want to?"

Lloyd turned around to stare at her in wonder. "What?"

Felicia stood up from the bed to sit on its edge. "I know I am not as sexy as my twin or anything. I want to have sex tonight. I am sure that even if I am as ugly as a toad, I'll still find a-"

Lloyd didn't know how he crossed the distance between him and Felicia. One minute he was at the door ready to leave, and at the next, he found Felicia in his arms pressed against the wall. He clenched his teeth tightly. This was getting too odd. Trying to stay away from Felicia was proving more difficult than he would like to admit.

Later, he can think about ways to avoid her, but the young woman in his bed has to learn some lessons this minute. "You know you are an identical twin to her sister."

"I... I-"

He placed one hand around her while the other trailed the side of her face, from the side of her eye, down her rosy cheeks to her jaw and her slightly open lips. "That's means that if Francisca is sexy, then you are...sexy too."

Felicia's lips wobbled. "Oh...so you didn't because you are professional."

"Fuck all that!" Lloyd descended on her lips with the vengeance of a deprived man. As his lips covered hers, he lost every bit of restraint he had. The way her lips met his was pure ecstasy. He felt her hands on his chest, and well- he lost it. He burned for her everything as his lips bamboozled her mouth. There was no mercy as he took and gave pleasure.

He heard her groan and pull her close against him, and that messed with his mind. How can he feel like a teenage boy kissing a woman for the first time? His shirt came off in a flash, and Felicia licked her top and bottom lips one after the other while trailing a finger over his chest to his navel.

"You are beautiful."

"Felicia," he called her name and took a step away from her."

"Uh?" She looked up at him.

"Tell me to leave right now," he said, briefly closing his eyes.

"Why?"

"Because if I don't stop right now. I won't be able to stop later."

Felicia smiled, closing the distance between them once again. "And who said anything about stopping?"

That was all he needed to hear. He carried Felicia in his arms and laid her gently on the bed. Then He pulled off his trousers and boxers so that he was kneeling over her in all his glory. He saw her eyes grow wide with shock as she gazed at his body from his head down to his toe, lingering her gaze at his torso.

The way she looked at him would be his undoing. She started taking off her clothes, but he stopped her. There was no need to rush. Felicia might have started this, but this would go at the pace he wanted.

He used his kneels to separate her thighs, then he unzipped her Jeans so that he could see her pink lacy panties. He placed kisses on her through the fabric, and she wiggled closer to his mouth for more. He kissed and suckled.

He pulled down the Jean to give more room, then he parted the fabric slightly so that her clits were exposed to him. She was wet! Wet with desire for him. He continued the onslaught of her woman lips, kissing and suckling. Until he felt her tense around him.

He raised his head and leaned over her top. He placed kisses on her ears and around it. Lloyd felt her hands in his hair as he moved to her full breast, suckling on one nipple after the other.

"I want more..."

Lloyd heard her and knew exactly how he felt. He pulled down her panties. Now she was fully exposed to him. Lloyd reached for his trousers and pulled out a condom.

He pulled it over him, then dipped a finger into her wet warmth. Lloyd was shocked to see how ready she was for him, and he couldn't wait any longer. He pulled her into his arms and kissed her. Then he gently eased himself into her warmth.

Felicia's groaned against him, pulling him against her. Lloyd's head was on cloud nine. She was right and yet ready for him.

But- she was too tight. There was something wrong, but before his brain could make out what was wrong, Felicia wrapped her legs against him, pulling him deeper against her, and he was done, for he plunged into her. That was when he realized what was wrong, but his brain didn't have time to think.

Her soft gasp against him was the only indication. She wrapped her legs around him, meeting every single thrust with her own. He would have stopped, but her body arched against his, asking for more. Her eyes were closed, and her face was etched with ecstasy.

He felt his body and hers tighten at the same time. He didn't rush Felicia. Instead, he matched her pace. Together, body against body, they both gave into its ecstasy when the storm came. Lloyd held her tightly against him as his body sagged in relief.

For a minute, they just lay like that without saying anything. Lloyd wanted to talk, but he saw that she had fallen asleep. Maybe this moment wasn't too perfect for words. He thought as he closed his eyes and held her closer against him.

Fortunately, Felicia felt perfect against the arc in his elbow.

***

Felicia woke up to the pang of hunger and the rays of the morning sun seeping through the window. She stretched, rolled, and found herself touching a hard surface. Slowly, she glanced up to notice Lloyd staring back at her.

"Hi," she chuckled nervously, tearing her gaze from his and

looking at everywhere in the room but at him.

"Hi," he said, holding her tightly against his chest. "About last night...it was amazing."

Surprised, she looked back at him and smiled shyly. She couldn't understand how any woman could look any man in the face after they made love. Maybe the way he glowed after a night of lovemaking makes every type of embarrassment disappear.

"I don't...I mean...what I want to ask is-" He stuttered uneasily.

Is there something cute and crazily affectionate about a grown-ass man when he acts like a baby around you? Felicia chuckled as she shamelessly watched him, trying to find the right words.

"You were a virgin!" He blurted out.

"You didn't like that?" She asked, her bravado disappearing.

Lloyd waved his hand quickly in disagreement. "That's not what I meant. I was surprised that...you know I am a stranger, and you gave me your virginity " he bit his lips as a thoughtful look appeared over his face. "I don't understand why you would give me something so special."

"I did because I wanted to. There was no other reason," Felicia answered matter of fact. "I was ready to lose it, and I did."

He touched her face gently. "I don't deserve you" he gently kissed her head. "But you drive me insane."

"That is good then because you also drive me crazy, but I am hungry!"

Lloyd blinked. "You ate just once yesterday."

"You didn't eat at all," she pointed out.

"Let's order room service," he suggested. "Now that you mentioned it. I realized that I am famished."

He asked her what she wanted to eat, then reached for the landline and placed their other. "They said it would take fifteen minutes."

"I think I should take my bath before they come back with the food."

"You are right, let's both do that" he stood up and headed for the bathroom.

Felicia couldn't stop staring. Her mouth suddenly went dry as she swallowed hard. Last night she had seen Lloyd under the night light, but today was different. He was gorgeous perfection, and artistic structure was shone vividly in all its glory.

Her heart seemed to be running in overdrive, she placed a hand over her chest, and the occupation thumping of her heart could move her hands. She was losing it where Lloyd was concerned.

"Aren't you taking your bath?" Lloyd peeled out of the bathroom door. "Or you don't want to bath with me?"

"What? I mean...of course. We could wash each other's back," she answered breathlessly.

He nods. "Good idea"

Felicia hurried out of bed, picked up a robe, and threw it over her body. Then she headed for the bathroom. Lloyd was already under the shower when she got in. She couldn't stop staring.

"Stop looking like that. It makes me think you have bad intentions" he chuckled lightly.

Felicia caught herself. "How? I wasn't doing anything," she said, feigning ignorance.

"Of course, you weren't. But if you were thinking about things you shouldn't be thinking about, don't. Nothing is going to happen."

"But why" she couldn't stop herself from asking.

He pulled her under the water and gave her a light kiss on the forehead. "Because I wasn't gentle last night, and your body needs time to heal."

She grumbled her disappointment. There were many things she wanted to do to Lloyd's body.

"You look disappointed," he mused, trying not to laugh.

She jerked her head up and frowned. "No!" She picked up a bar of soap and rubbed it against his chest. "I am not disappointed in the least but are you sure that you are a man of your word?"

"Yeah!" He scoffed proudly.

"Good" she bit her bottom lips and pointedly but slowly turned her gaze to his bulging part, standing erect in front of her.

Felix groaned but smiled dangerously. He placed a finger under her chin so that she would face him. "I am a man of my words, don't mind Lloyd junior because I control Lloyd junior."

Felix held the shower in his hand and let the waterfall on his head for a few minutes. "I think I am done here. Take your time. I will be outside."

After he spoke his mind, Felicia also tried to talk, but he had already left walked out of the bathroom. She scowled at his retreating figure, her mouth hanging in shock as her shoulder dropped. She hadn't actually expected him to leave. She turned on the shower and let the waterfall over her body, cooling her already headed skin.

CHAPTER SEVEN

Lloyd had suggested that they take a tour around Soho instead of going back to the apartment, and Felicia agreed. She figured Lloyd didn't want to be alone in a room with her. Yes, she was disappointed but was excited to see the city.

First things first, they went shopping for clothes. Since they hadn't planned on staying the night, they didn't have extra clothing.

There were brands on every single corner Felicia didn't know what to pick, from Zara, Chanel, Brandy Melville, and so much more. There were in Broadway Street where a lot of high-end boutiques.

"Are we going into any of these shops, or are you going to continue gawking?" Lloyd rolled his eyes as if he were saying, 'Woman!'

Felicia made a face at him and pouted with a silly expression. "Fine, let's go into that one."

As he followed closely behind her, Lloyd seemed to be hiding a smile. They walked into the boutique and selected the clothing they required. After four hours, Felicia left the boutique with four shopping gift bags, while Lloyd only received one.

"Why do women always need all that number of clothes," Lloyd asked once they got back to the hotel.

Lloyd was changing to his new outfit as he spoke. All day, he had tried his best to stay away from Felicia; he was always catching himself staring at her while his mind imagined all the things he could do to her body.

Intentionally he had gone to his room to change because he couldn't trust himself around her, and yet the woman had the audacity to call herself plain!

"Felicia, are you through? If we want to enjoy the sights, it would be better to leave now," he called, but no one answered.

He sometimes muttered about women and time to himself, then headed to her room to hasten her. He lightly knocked on her door but didn't get any reply, then he placed his ear against the door but didn't hear any sound coming from the room.

He knocked two more times but didn't still get an answer.

"I am coming in" Lloyd turned the doorknob and cautiously entered Felicia's room. A sense of urgency hit him as he entered the room; she wasn't inside. He turned around to check behind the door, but he was a little too late.

The door was shut in his face, and as he launched to attack the perpetrator, he saw that it was Felicia laced in wicked black laced lingerie. Lloyd was sure his brain short-circuited for a second or a minute because he was tongue-tied with the image in front of him

Her nipples were pointed hard under the lace material that did nothing to hide the full breast that it held. Lloyd's mouth watered, and he imagined his lips around her bud, sucking on her sweetness. He shook his head and slapped his face. No, he should get out of this room. He had told himself that yesterday that what happened was a mistake that wouldn't repeat itself, but now he couldn't tear his gaze away from her.

The wicked smile on her face told him that she knew exactly what she was doing. But he told himself, he is a man, a police officer. He can resist her, and he will resist this woman right in front of him.

Beads of sweat gathered on his forehead as he tried to rear his gaze away from her. He told himself that the only thing he had to do was open the door and leave the room while making sure he didn't come in contact with her in the slightest because every time he touched her. He burned for more.

So he used his combat training to sidestep away from Felicia, who was leaning against the wall beside the door with a devilish grin on her face.

Without any trouble, Lloyd found the doorknob and opened the door. He turned to look at Felicia to see her reaction, but she still hadn't moved from the wall. He opened the door, stepped outside the room, and closed the door behind him, but he was surprised.

This wasn't the reaction he had expected.

He turned around, opened Felicia's door again, and stepped back inside, but his hand was still on the knob in case he wanted to run away.

"Aren't you going to stop me?"

Felicia looked up from her finger and shrugged. "No"

"What?"

"Men are funny," She scoffed and tapped his open expanse on his chest with a dainty finger. "I have told you what I wanted many times, and no, I won't run after a man. Even one as sexy as you!"

"So, you think I am sexy" Lloyd couldn't help the grin on his face.

Felicia let out a breath as if she were tired. "That's beside the point. What I want you to know is that. If you don't make a move towards me. I won't force you. We don't want people thinking that I am sexually harassing you. Do we?"

Lloyd grabbed the finger tapping his chest, and Felicia stopped. They were a shadow in her eyes, but he couldn't read her expression.

"You are right."

"What?" Felicia's head shot up.

Lloyd couldn't help but smile. He brought Felicia's finger to his to the opening on his lips and paused. He saw her catch her breath, and he smiled to himself. Then he sucked on the finger. It was a small act, but the groan that escaped Felicia's lips was going things to his body.

He pulled her agonist his body. "Can you see what you do to me? You make me crazy, and I lose my senses."

"And is that a good or bad thing," Felicia asked breathlessly.

"Bad, definitely bad" He groaned and pulled her more closely against his body. "I feel like I am taking advantage of you. You were a virgin."

"Because I wanted to be a virgin, and no, I am not a kid. I am twenty-five, and I know what I want, and I want you!"

"Good" he bent his head to a full bud. "Because I am very thirsty."

Before Felicia could react, Lloyd had one nipple in his mouth. He was suckling on it through her lace-like a hungry baby, while his other hand circled and teased the other breast.

Felicia squirmed and groaned with pleasure under his hand. She put her hand on his head and brought his head closer to her as if she couldn't get enough of him. He left the first bud and focused on the second bud.

Felicia could feel her leg going weak, so she leaned back on the wall and let Lloyd work his magic. She wished he would go on forever. She had watched porn videos and gotten turned on, but she had never thought that she could feel this type of heaven in her wildest dream.

She felt in control, and there was no shame in how she was feeling. She knew that if there was a mirror and she saw her reflection. She would probably not recognize herself. Suddenly, she placed a hand under Lloyd's face to look at her.

"I want to try something," Felicia told him calmly and pulled him to his feet. Lloyd couldn't understand what she was about to do, but he followed her lid. She took him to the bed and gently laid him on the bed.

"What are you up to?" He raised in brows in question.

Felicia smiled wickedly and climbed on top of the bed so that she was seated over his torso. She saw him gulp hard and felt powerful, then she placed her finger under his shirt and pulled it up.

Then she leaned over his nipple and kissed him. Sucking on his smaller nipple, the same way he had done with her, using her tongue to nibble, circle, and bite gently on the sensitive flesh.

She heard a sound like a cry and was surprised to find out that it was coming from Lloyd. She raised it down to her head to find him looking at her dangerously. He grabbed her head and brought it down to his face, and kissed her.

No, this kiss was like a punishment. Lloyd was taking no prisoners. He kissed her bottom lips and thrust his tongue inside her mouth to savor her mouth. When Felicia was certain that she couldn't take anymore, she felt Lloyd's hand trailing down her navel and into her panties.

He teased and controlled her center; she was holding him tightly at this point. His fingers were going in and out in a rhythm movement, and her body moved with his fingers. Meeting him for every single thrust.

"I want you!" she cried as he felt herself coming.

Lloyd wasn't done with her yet. He pulled himself off the bed and pulled her to the edge of the bed. Such that, she was seated on its edge. Then he knelt between her thighs pulled down her lacy panties. He bit his bottom lips and stared at her for a few seconds before bringing his lips to her center.

Wait, what? Was him? No, he couldn't. Felicia's question was answered the moment the sensation went from Lloyd's lips to her clits and brain.

She gasped loudly. It was, in a way, painful, but it was pleasurable. This was insane. She brought her hands to tell him to stop but found her fingers in his hair, pulling him closer to her sex.

"What are you doing to me?" Felicia cried as her body shook with ecstasy, and she fell back on the bed.

She ran her fingers through her hair, signing with pleasure. From the corner of her eyes, she saw Lloyd taking off his trousers, and another mischievous idea flashed through her devilish mind.

Quickly before Lloyd could react, she pushed him against the bed and stood over him.

"What are you up to again?" He asked, a shadow over his eyes.

"Something you will love if I get right and if I get it wrong...." Felicia knelt in front of Lloyd and stared pointy at his man's length, and gulped hard. Then she took it in her hand, as she had seen in the videos she had watched. Run her fingers through its length. Then she put it in his mouth!

Lloyd almost jumped out of bed. She followed the routine she had seen and took him deep into her mouth. In and out. Repeating the motion while Lloyd buckled under her hand. She heard different words coming out of his mouth, but nothing made sense.

"Are you trying to kill me?" Lloyd groaned.

Felicia looked up in shock. "Wait, don't you like that?"

Lloyd bit his button lips and laughed. "Of course, I do."

He stood up gently and placed her on the bed as if she was fine China. Then he picked up his trousers and brought out a condom. Felicia was tempted to ask him what he was doing with a condom if he wasn't going to have sex with her, but he entered her wetness, and she felt his entire length inside her. She lost all train of thought.

Instead, she wrapped her legs tightly against him and followed him thrust for thrust on a journey to find ecstasy.

***

Felicia woke up later in the evening. Her whole body was entwined with Lloyd's body and legs joined together at every point. The smell of masculinity filled the air, and the sound of his heartbeat against her ear was like soothing music to her ear.

She looked up at the face of the man sleeping in her arms and felt a sense of contentment.

She might not be in love with Lloyd, but this moment was where she would rather be.

CHAPTER EIGHT

The next day, both Lloyd and Felicia unanimously decided to stay back in Soho for a few more days. They didn't want to stay away from one another, and it was obvious.

Felicia wanted to stay in the hotel room and have sex all day, but Lloyd suggested sightseeing. Felicia was torn; the only sight she wanted to explore was the architectural design called Lloyd

But Lloyd insisted, so they visited the one-world observatory, and despite her earlier judgment, she loved it. Everything was a first for Felicia. She had schooled in London, from her prep to her university days. She had worked as the COO for Smith Co in London. She had never really traveled unless you want to count the time she traveled to Paris with her sister as a young girl when they visited their grandparents.

She had seen pictures of the observatory, but nothing did its justice. From the hundredth floor, she could see different towns. Lloyd pointed out Manhattan, Brooklyn Bride view, New Jersey, and other surrounding waters. Everything seemed so small from that height.

The view of the 9/11 memorial pools seems more solemn from that height. Felicia walked fast like a child, excited to see what was next. Finally, they got to the top floor. Felicia didn't know that she could be more amazed by nature. She looked through the observatory and giggled like a baby, pulling Lloyd along with her so that he could also see it.

"Isn't it beautiful, Lloyd?" She asked eagerly.

"Very beautiful," he said but was staring at her.

Felicia noticed what he was doing and couldn't stop blushing. Tired and famished, they headed back down to a diner opposite the street to have lunch.

The dinner was owned by a young Italian man in his late thirties, Ray. At first, Felicia thought he was a waiter or manager until he introduced himself. She couldn't hide her surprise but seeing him also made her remember how much she loved working at Smith Co.

Ray led them to a seat near the giant television screen, but Lloyd politely told Ray that he preferred the chair beside the window. Ray didn't argue or ask questions; instead, he led them to a seat near the transparent glass that saw the whole street.

Felicia knew why Ray had suggested the chairs beside the television on settling down. The occasional honking of cars and the noise of passerby was intense in this part of the room. Ray took their order and left them alone.

She whispered, "Can we change seats, please?"

"I am afraid not. I prefer this side so that I can see who is coming and going out of this place," he said softly but unapologetically.

"Oh," she sighed, funny she had forgotten why and how she had met Lloyd. He was just an officer assigned to protect her, and he was doing her job. The reminder pissed her that she would like to admit it. "I forgot; you were doing your job."

"Are you angry about something?" He asked without breaking eye contact with her.

"No, nothing"

He sighed. "Just say it already."

She shot him a glare. "It's nothing. I don't know how to explain it myself" she was telling the truth. She didn't know how she felt. She wasn't sad or happy. She was in a funk and didn't know how she got into it.

"So, something is wrong?"

"I-"

"Here you go," Ray returned with the food, Spaghetti for Lloyd and medium steak and yogurt for Felicia. "I am sorry for the slow service. My part-time is late again."

Felicia smiled. "Don't worry about it. It wasn't even late in the slightest" she stared at the plate of food in front of her and was amazed at its artistic plating. She had eaten in some fine establishment back in the UK, and they weren't even this dope. "This looks like a million buck."

"Thank you," Ray said, his eyes brimming as if he had just won a lottery. "You guys look alike. Are you siblings?

Felicia opened her mouth after she heard the question. She glanced from Ray to Lloyd and back to Ray, her mouth still agape. She kicked Lloyd under the table. "He is asking you a question. It is rude not to answer."

Lloyd looked up from his spaghetti. He had already started eating as soon as the plates touched the table. "What do you what me to say?"

"Answer his question."

"She is my..." Lloyd smiled mischievously, lowering his eyes so she was on eye level. "She is my sister."

Ray smiled sheepishly. "Wow, what a beautiful combination. The both of you."

Felicia couldn't believe what she heard. Was he denying her now? Is he making marking the line they shouldn't cross? She scoffed. What was she expecting? She had personally told him that she was mature, that both of them could have casual sex.

She picked up the fork and dug into her steak.

Hmm, it tastes sweet. Felicia thought through clenched jaws. She felt someone persistently tapping her shoulder. She jerked her head up in anger.

"What!"

"I am so sorry. I didn't mean to disturb you," Ray said apologetically.

Felicia took a deep breath and waved her hands quickly. "I am sorry, I didn't mean to snap at you. I am very sorry," she swore. Honestly, she hadn't meant to shout at the man. Instead, she had been so deep in her thoughts that she hadn't expected him to tap her.

"No problem," Ray assured, then he pointed to the opposite end of the diner where a man in his late twenties or early thirties sat, smiling at them. "He told me to tell you to go tell you that you are beautiful, and he would love to know you."

Felicia blinked. Taken aback, she pointed at herself to confirm that Ray was talking about her. "You mean me?"

"Yes," Ray nodded.

"Can you believe this Lloyd, he-" she stopped talking when she saw the nonchalant look in his eyes. He had called her a sibling. Fine! That's how she would treat him. "Brother?"

Lloyd raised his brow. "You are talking to me?"

She nodded enthusiastically. "Can I have the phone number?" She asked as innocently as a cat.

"Phone number? It is for an emergency, and you know that" his voice low with a hint of anger.

"This," she pointed at Ray. "...is an emergency, your sister is going to get a boyfriend. So please give Ray the number so that he can give it to that handsome man over there."

Lloyd scoffed as if he couldn't believe what he heard, but he licked its lips and shrugged. He picked up a paper tissue signaled for Ray to give him a pen. Ray handed over the pen in his overalls to Lloyd.

"Here, this is the number" He turned the paper over to Felicia.

"Thanks" she grabbed it without hesitation and handed it over to Ray. "Tell them that he can call me whenever he wants. I would love to hear from him"

Ray collected the tissue from Felicia and smiled thankfully. "You guys are just like my younger brother and me. We bicker and fight all the time, but we love one another."

"You hear that?" Felicia cocked her head to one side playfully. "We look like the perfect siblings.

Lloyd started talking but folded his lips in, shook his head, and continued to dig into the spaghetti. He looked like he was enjoying his meal a little too much. Felicia was pissed. The fact that he didn't look angry or unbothered was infuriating. She tried to hide her feeling, put on her best poker face, and faced her food.

She looked up till she finished every single bite. She picked up her yogurt and sipped it gently. She felt his gaze upon her and didn't want to feel like a chicken, so she peered her eyes upwards to look at Lloyd. Her eyes were definitely saying, 'What can I do for you?"

She found him holding a glass of water in one hand and her meds in the other hand. She knew he cared about her well-being only because it was his job and nothing more. She was the one that said they were mature, she thought to herself for the second time that day. So why was she expecting more from someone that couldn't give it to her?

Felicia grabbed the meds out of his hands without saying a word. She downed the pills and water like a pro smiled sarcastically at her protector. She bent her head from his gaze again and focused on her yogurt.

Felicia wanted to continue giving him the silent treatment, but she couldn't continue for her life. She loved hearing him talk.

"I realized I don't know anything about you," she said, still not looking at him.

"You know everything there is to know about me," came his deep Authoritative voice.

More infuriated, she glanced up at him, her eyes burning with anger. "You are a police officer, so I bet you know everything there is to know about me, but I know nothing about you except that your name is Lloyd Dean. A police officer who is too good looking for his own good!"

Sometimes Felicia shocked herself when she closed her hand over her mouth after the last sentence. It seems that she is always catching herself in embarrassing situations where Lloyd is concerned.

"Don't bother to answer. I seem to be forcing you to do things with me" Felicia sighed and continued to look down at the table.

Lloyd placed a hand over hers, making her look at him again. "What gave you that idea that you can force me to do anything?" He asked softly. One finger trailed over Felicia's hand. "I just didn't think that you would really want to know anything about me."

Felicia licked her lips, realizing all her resentment towards him had disappeared as soon as he started speaking to her.

" I am a policeman and -"

"I know that!"

"Can I talk?" He chuckled.

Felicia bit her lips and didn't interrupt again; at least he changed his mind and stopped talking. She imitated that she was closing a zip on her lips with her fingers and threw away the key.

He smiled again at her awkward acting. "As I was saying, I am a policeman, from a family of a policeman-"

"Your father was a policeman? Wow, that is like a family business -" she saw Lloyd's reaction too late. She chuckled nervously and re-zipped her lips.

Lloyd sighed and rolled his eyes as if he meant that there was nothing he could do to her. "No, my father is not a policeman. My mother is the police officer" Lloyd paused to take a sip of water.

Felicia's eyes grew at Lloyd's statement, she had so many questions, but she zipped her lips tightly. She has tested Lloyd's patience for too long. He might just decide not to say anything else if she as much as coughed.

"You are right. I am from a family of cops but from my mother's side of the family. Her father was a commissioner before he retired, and so was his father before him. When my grandma only had my mother a woman, he thought the family tradition would disappear. He was wrong because my mother is an assistant chief of police at the moment, and I am a lieutenant."

"Wow," she looked at him proudly in a new light. "Isn't like a big deal? I mean lieutenant? Why are you babying me when you are a hotshot?"

A shadow flashed over Lloyd's face but disappeared almost as soon as it appeared, making Felicia rethink that she must have imagined it.

"Firstly, I have a boss, and your dad is a big hotshot, and that concludes why I am here" he shot a sly smile in her direction.

"You got babysitting duties when you would rather be doing other things," Felicia sighed in exaggeration. "I understand."

"You are funny," he sighed. "I am the second child of three children. My elder brother, who is a Director in my dad's company, and my younger sister, who is studying fashion designing."

"You sound like you love them"

"Of course, I do, even when they act crazy and make me mad for no reason. I still love them a lot," he answered proudly, smiling as if he just remembered a fond memory. "And there you have it. There is nothing special about me."

"If you say that there is nothing special about you, then there is nothing I can say about that," she joked, then a sly smile appeared over her lips. "I have one question."

"I am scared already." He tried to hide a smile. "Anytime you have that look on your face. I get into trouble."

Felicia couldn't help herself; she was beside herself with laughter, but after a few minutes. She controlled herself and stopped laughing.

"I want to ask if you are dating anyone" Felicia met his gaze. "I know that we didn't define our relationship, but I just feel like knowing."

Lloyd gazed into Felicia's eyes for a few seconds, smiled, and held her hand once more. "No, I am not dating anyone right now, and we define our relationship."

Felicia raised a brow.

"I don't do casual sex, ever."

"You w-what…"

Ring!

The phone ringing interrupted Felicia.

"Hold that thought," Lloyd said as he picked up the phone. Once he saw the name on the caller, his demeanor changed. "Give me a minute. I need to take this call," he said, raising a finger to her as he excused himself.

Felicia watched as he hurried out of the restaurant. She didn't need to read minds to know that something was wrong. She tried to think of what could have gone wrong, but her mind couldn't think of anything. It could be a family or work issue, but she wasn't close to him to assume what could have gone amiss. The only thing she could do was wait for him to come back and give her the news.

Waiting has never been Felicia's strong suit. Although Lloyd had been gone for just a few minutes, it felt more like hours. She noticed that she was tapping her feet impatiently, but she couldn't stop.

A smile spread over her face when she saw him coming back to their table. She searched his face for answers, but he was hard to read.

"What happened? It doesn't look like good news," She asked as soon as he took his seat opposite her.

"You are right. It wasn't good news," Lloyd answered without looking her in the eye.

"Then what happened?" She pushed. Her heart felt like it was on pause as she eagerly waited for an answer.

"Do you want the bad news or the worst news?" he asked, cringing as he spoke.

She stood up hastily. "Two bad news!" Felicia shouted. She turned her face in embarrassment when she noticed that she was carrying a scene and sat back down. "Spill both"

Lloyd held Felicia's hand across the table, gently trailing a finger over it. "The media got wind of the serial killer and published the names of the people he has killed, and your name was included, " Lloyd said softly, looking at her intensely to see her reaction.

"People didn't know before, right?"

"Yeah, and that is not the worst news" Lloyd held Felicia's hand tightly across the table.

Felicia tried to steady her hands, but she shook from head to toe. She was on tenterhook waiting for him to speak.

"There is a new victim. The wedding psychopath killed a new victim."

The whole world came to a stop.

Felicia pulled her hands from Lloyd's hold. Numb and dazed with a truckload of anger. That coward had killed some other woman. Felicia knew she was supposed to be the next victim, but she had escaped because of their father's meticulously planned.

What did that scary man say he wanted from his victims? Felicia glared. He wanted all his victims to get married, right? Well, she wouldn't give him the satisfaction. She turned her gaze towards Lloyd, who looked concerned with the wires he could see turning in her head.

The holiday is over, and the heart is closed until further notice. She might have been crazy about Lloyd because of his looks and personality, but that ends now. She would stay away from him because she would never fall in love or marry.

Felicia clenched her teeth, swearing silently. That wedding psychopath won't win because she won't let him! She might be developing feelings for Lloyd, but remembering all the heartbreak and tears her family had shed because of this excuse of a human being was infuriating.

She would have to break this thing with Lloyd. That was the end of the honeymoon.

CHAPTER NINE

How can one person change overnight? That was the question running through Lloyd's mind when he picked up the grocery from the local mart. He paid the cashier, Andrew, and headed out of the shop.

"You forgot your change," Andrew called from behind the counter.

Lloyd stopped in his tracks and headed back to meet him. "Thanks, Andrew, you are the only one I trust in Battery Park" he smiled and collected his change from the young man.

"I am the only one you trust? What about your sister?" Andrew winked suggestively. "I have asked you to introduce me to her for the past one month, but you haven't."

Lloyd forced a smile. "She never listens to me, Andrew. You know how sisters are,"

Lloyd didn't wait to hear any more from Andrew. He picked the change and headed out of the mart. The house was a block away, so I hadn't taken the car out. He needed to think. After that day at that diner in Soho, Felicia had utterly changed.

How she changed in the space of two months was too much. She wasn't like the woman who had asked him to kiss her and made love to him, a total stranger. Instead, she suggested returning to Battery Park that evening despite their previous plans to explore other parts of New York.

The look in her eyes had told him not to argue with her. So that night, they had returned back to Battery Park. He tried to talk to her, to understand how she felt and if he could help, but she had built an impenetrable wall around her so that no one could come close to break it.

He missed her smile and their lovemaking. What he had with her was the best sex he had ever had with anyone, and the memory of that night was etched in his soul. But Felicia seemed determined to prevent that night from happening ever again. She would disappear from any room as soon as she found him there.

They never spoke except the occasional pleasantries when they met in the kitchen or when she went for her morning jog. She avoided him like the plague. Lloyd didn't want to admit it, but it bothered him.

The nights he had spent in Soho with her were the last in a while where he slept peacefully. He had gone to the pharmacy to get his prescription before going to the mart. He needed an extra dosage to fall asleep, but he found himself waking up within two to four hours even when he slept. He was tired and missed Felicia.

He glanced up and realized that he had gotten to the front of the house. He climbed the stairs and headed for the kitchen while he strained his ear to know if she was around, but the house was dead silent. He put the grocery away in the cabinet above and headed out of the kitchen.

"Ah," Lloyd yelped in pain. It all happened in a split second. Lloyd had a head butt with Felicia. He hadn't seen her. It was as if she had come out of nowhere.

He saw her holding her head in pain and moved his hands to rub her forehead, but she stepped back, away from him instinctively. The pain that flashed through his chest was something he had expected.

"I wasn't trying to hurt you or anything" he pushed past her angrily, heading out of the kitchen. "I won't eat you because I touch you."

"I didn't- " she started talking.

Lloyd raised his hand to stop her excuses. "Forget it, Felicia, sorry, I didn't mean to hurt you," he apologized, but he couldn't hide his anger as he strode out of the house.

As soon as he opened the door, Lloyd stood in shock at the figure in front of him about to hit the doorbell.

"What are you doing here, Andrew? Lloyd asked the cashier.

Andrew smoked sheepishly. "I finally got a chance to speak to Felicia one, and she agreed to go out with me. I am here to pick her up."

Something sparked in Lloyd's head. He glanced back into the house to see that Felicia looked ready to go out. He hadn't noticed that before because he had bumped into her."

"When did you see her?" He felt obliged to ask for some reason.

"A few minutes ago," came the proud reply.

Lloyd tried to make sense of the situation, but his head hurt like a hammer was constantly hit on it. He closed his eyes took a deep breath, but it did nothing to alleviate the pain.

Finally, he opened his eyes and relaxed his teeth and hands. "Have a great time," he told Andrew and stormed out of the street. He needed to get away from Felicia. If he stayed one more minute in front of Andrew, he might hit the man in the face, and he wouldn't be able to explain his reasons to anyone.

He broke into a run. The spring is an excellent time to exercise.

***

Felicia swallowed and released the breath she hadn't realized that she was holding. She had the dark and dangerous gaze Lloyd had turned her way, and this time she was sure she hadn't imagined it.

She hadn't intentionally gotten him angry, but she was a man - woman of her words. She planned to keep her promise to herself but living with the hottest man she knew alive made it more complicated than she had bargained. Fortunately, she had been allowed a phone a month ago, unless she would have gone mad with unresolved, pent-up sexual feelings and boredom.

Today, she had taken a sneak peek to see her family on social media and saw that they seemed to be doing fine, too fine, actually. It looked like they had moved on and forgotten about her. She told herself that was what she wanted, but seeing her mother, father, sister, and brother-in-law laughing without her in the video did something to her head.

Guess she was human after all.

She was happy for them sincerely, she was, but she was the one with that life, not Fran. She was the one who stayed when Fran had run away from home. She was the one who helped pick up the pieces of the family. She was the one who showed up to help her mother plan parties and the one whose only dream was to build the family company across several continents. Now it seemed like Fran was living her life, and she was replaced by her twin sister.

Felicia felt shitty, but she could help the way she felt. So, when Andrew had suggested they go out on a date, she had accepted without hesitation. She needed something to take her mind off her petty self-pity.

"Are you ready?" Andrew's voice broke through her review.

"Oh, yes. Sorry" Felicia answered hurriedly. "So, where are you taking me?"

Andrew smiled sheepishly, blushing. "It is a surprise."

"Surprise?" she waved her hand excitedly with a forced smile. She was already regretting this but couldn't back out now. She sighed and quickly scanned the street to see if he could find Lloyd, but no matter how she scanned the neighborhood, she didn't see any sight of him.

"Ready" Andrew slightly bowed and directed her out of the house with his hands. "I borrowed my uncle's truck. I hope it is comfortable."

Felicia couldn't help but smile at his innocence. He was cute and not bad-looking herself. If only her heart wasn't taken by another. Felicia quickly shook her head to dismiss her last thought. She had no feelings for Lloyd, she reminded herself. All. She felt for that hunk was sex.

She grabbed Andrew's hand with purpose as he led her to the red truck parked in her driveway. As she settled beside the excited man, she reminded herself that Friday would be a long one.

***

Whatever Felicia had thought about, this was wider than her imagination. She had felt Andrew would take her to a fancy restaurant, where they would talk about themselves for a few minutes, say goodbye at the end of the day, and that would be the end of it. Staring at the lake from the ferry as it drove towards the Statue of Liberty, she began to think differently.

The view of the four hundred and fifty thousand pounds and one hundred- and a two-feet tall statue standing in all its glory was enough to make her catch her breath. To believe that this was a gift of goodwill from France to America was also unbelievable.

If she knew that she was going to the statue of liberty, she would have brought her camera, but since the gadget wasn't with her. She pulled out her phone and took a picture of the masterpiece.

As soon as the ferry docked on Liberty Island, Andrew helped her off the boat with a promise of more to come.

"I promise you would love everything about today," he swore childishly.

Felicia wanted to smack herself. Andrew should be in his late twenties. Why was she comparing him to a child? She was twenty-five and likely younger than the man. A picture of Lloyd came to her mind, and she groaned in frustration. The cause of her diverted thoughts!

Instead of thinking of Lloyd, she focused on the expanse of land around her, the smell of the water around her. Still, as soon as she stepped into the presence of the woman holding the torch, she felt a little sad. She wished she was out with Lloyd, sightseeing and having a good time with him.

She was suddenly curious about what he was up to. She wished that he was fine, doing whatever he liked. The whole day went like a blur. She wasn't as excited as she thought she would be. Andrew had gotten hot dogs and French fries later, and that was all she could remember about her trip to Liberty Island.

She tried to smile for Andrew but her cheeks hurt from laughing and smiling at his jokes all day. Andrew seemed excited, and nothing could dampen his mood as he took pictures of the statue and her.

Felicia watched Andrew and wished she could live carefree as he did, but she couldn't, or could she?

***

Felicia got back home late that night. Earlier, Andrew had tried to steal a kiss at the end of their date, but she unconsciously turned her face away. He looked disappointed for a few seconds but apologized. After another few seconds, he looked like his jovial self once again.

"You are already in love with someone else and don't have a place for me in your heart," Andrew told her when he dropped her at home.

Felicia had denied it vehemently. "No, there is no such person!"

Andrew just laughed. "Let me see you go in."

Felicia slid her keys into the keyhole, opened the door but turned around to wave at Andrew before she finally headed inside the house. As soon as she closed the door, she heard the sound of his truck driving off.

The lights were switched off, and I didn't bother turning it back on. Instead, Felicia took off her shoes and tiptoed up the now familiar stairs so as not to wake Lloyd up. She heaves a smile of relief when she got in front of her without any accident and opened her door, which squeaked softly as she tried to open it.

She tiptoed carefully into the room and gently closed the door behind her, but she stopped at the last minute when she heard Lloyd's voice from the room opposite her. She turned her ear towards his room to ensure she didn't imagine the noise. The voice didn't repeat itself, so she started closing the door again, but as she was about to close the door again. She heard a fearful scream from Lloyd's room.

She didn't think twice. Her legs worked faster than her brain. One minute she was inside her room, and the next, she was inside Lloyd's room. He was sleeping but groaning without waking up, with sweats covering him from head to toe.

"No... please don't do it," he cried, throwing his hands as if he was fighting with someone.

She was scared to see him like that, she bent over him to wake him up, but he fought while dreaming.

"No...leave them, I will do what you want, "He cried painfully, suddenly grabbing Felicia's hand as she tried to wake him. "I will do it. I will kill her. Just let everybody go," he added in defeat.

Felicia didn't know, which shocked her more. Lloyd became calm suddenly or the resigned look on his face when he said he would kill someone. He was still holding her, so she gently pried her hand out of his hold.

She noticed that his hand was slightly hot, not sure if that was because of her body temperature. She went out of the room, headed for the kitchen, and pulled out the first aid box from one of the top cabinets.

From the cabinet, she searched for the thermometer. As soon as she found it, she half flew up the stairs back into Lloyd's room. She placed the thermometer to his ear. Forty degrees was what the thermometer read. He was running a fever!

For a minute, her brain couldn't think. She stared in shock at Lloyd fast asleep, turning and groaning without waking up. She had to do something, she snapped out of her fear. Rushed to the bathroom picked up a bowl and a small towel.

She returned to his room and placed the cold towel over his forehead. She changed the towel every five minutes. Within and after an hour, she tested his temperature. She sighed in relief when she saw that his body temperature had reduced.

Felicia squeezed out the towel but still placed it over his head, then she settled on the chair opposite his bed to rest, but before she closed her eyes. She put her phone on a thirty minutes timer to wake her up every thirty minutes so that she could occasionally check upon him.

A pang of regret flashed through her as she watched him from the chair. If only she hadn't gone out today, she would have noticed that he wasn't feeling too well. Another voice in her head disapproved. She hadn't looked at Lloyd for once in the past two months.

She would likely not have noticed anything.

***

Lloyd tried to open his eyes, but his whole body felt heavy. He remembered the night before he had been feeling funny and had called John at the Pharmacy and told him to get some meds for him, but John had declined and told Lloyd that he wasn't going to give Lloyd any medications until he was certain that he was actually ill and not pretending.

After discovering that Lloyd was going through his sleeping pills like water, the old man didn't trust Lloyd with his meds. Lloyd had also thought it wasn't a big deal until this morning. His eyes felt hot and cold at the same time. He forced himself to open his eyes, and the first thing that caught his attention was Felicia sleeping opposite him in a chair curled like a cat.

This was a site he could wake up to every day. Even though he was happy to see her, he didn't understand what she was doing in his room. She shuddered from the morning cold, so he sat up to get her a cloth to cover her leg, but something wet fell on his face.

He was surprised to see that it was a face towel. Then he noticed the small bowl at the bottom of the chair below Felicia. A smile spread over his face, he wasn't sure if he was blushing, but he knew that he was grinning from ear to ear as he stared at her.

Standing up has never felt more like torture, but he forced himself to climb out of bed, picked the cover, pulled himself towards Felicia, and covered her. She turned in her sleep and opened her eyes.

Shock and recognition flashed in her eyes at the same time. "What are you doing up?" she half-shouted.

"I love the way you talk to me, "he chuckled on shaky legs.

"You have gone mad with fever" she stood up quickly, throwing the cover away from her body, and immediately helped him back to the bed.

"Lie down," she ordered as she bent over him.

"Your voice drives me crazy" Lloyd chuckled again but let her lay him back on the bed.

"You need food and your medicines," Felicia said more to herself than to Lloyd. "But I am a horrible cook, so I better order take out from Jake's

She first picked up her phone and ordered take-out from the

nearby Diner; after that, she called John at the pharmacy.

"Yes, his temperature was high yesterday, but it is now normal," She explained softly to the mouthpiece. "Ok, I should get the First aid box?"

Felicia went down to the kitchen, brought down the first aid box again, and headed up to Lloyd's room. "Yes, I can see the meds...we have everything, including paracetamol" She nodded to the phone as if John could see her. "I will give it to him after he eats," she promised.

"What did John say? "Lloyd asked, raising his head to get a better view of Felicia.

"He said he thought you were lying because you are abusing your sleeping pills, but he will check up on you in the evening." She answered, looking at him as she wanted to ask a question but stopped herself.

'Hmm," Lloyd shrugged nonchalantly.

"What happened? You were fine when I left you yesterday."

Lloyd frowned. Remembering that Felicia went out with Andrew still pissed him off. "So, did you have a nice time" he couldn't help but ask?

"That's not the question. I asked what happened yesterday" Felicia pushed, not letting him get away with changing the conservation.

"You had that much fun? You can talk to me about such kinds of stuff. I am your protector. I should know everything to know about you."

Felicia's eyes looked aflame with anger. She strolled up to the bed and pointed a finger in his face. "I don't need you or anyone else to protect; just because I am a girl doesn't mean that I automatically need protecting!"

Lloyd was surprised at her behavior. He hadn't meant anything by what he said. He only meant to say the truth. The only reason he was in New York was because of her. He was here to protect her, so why was she angry? Felicia was an enigma he could never understand. When he thinks he has seen one side of her, she changes like a chameleon, and he is lost once again.

The doorbell downstairs paused his thoughts as Felicia stopped glaring at him and went down the stairs. After a few minutes, she reappeared with a packaged food from Jake in front of him.

'Your food is ready," Felicia said as she unpacked it. "I will help up soon.

Lloyd wasn't that weak, so he sat upon his own; actually, he felt better already, but it seems like the only reason Felicia was in his room and speaking with him was because of his sickness, so he might as well go along with it.

He had missed her.

"Eat" Felicia placed a small stool in front of the bed and placed the food in front of Lloyd.

He frowned. "You are not nice or romantic. Can't you see that I am not feeling fine?"

"Fine, I will help you," She groaned. She sat down beside him on the bed and fed him a spoonful of porridge. "I'm I nice now?"

He shook his head. "You are supposed to blow my food and clean my mouth before and after feeding me!"

"You are not a baby!" she laughed, holding her sides.

Lloyd loved the sound of her throaty laughter. It filled his heart, and the heaviness he felt from her distance disappeared, but she could leave again as soon as he got better. He frowned again.

"Fine, see, I am blowing on the food. "Felicia blew on another spoonful of food when she was the frown on his face thinking that he was angry with her. "Here, take this too."

"This is the sweetest food I have ever tasted

Felicia rolled her eyes. "I know you love Jake's, but c'mon his can't be the sweetest you have tasted."

"It is because you fed it to me."

"Just eat for now and stop talking about silly things," Felicia said; she didn't look him in the eyes as she continued to feed him.

Lloyd didn't say anything but silently watched her feed him. The fact that such a simple act could make his heart feel fuller was crazy. Felicia finished feeding him the porridge and handed over a bunch of pills to him.

Dutifully as a baby, he down everything in one swallow.

"I will check on you later," she said as she packed the dirty plates together. "For now, sleep and let the meds take effect."

"You are going?" he asked, holding her hand suddenly; since she wasn't expecting him to have her, she trips and falls on his chest. He was still sitting, but he held her against him. "Why are you leaving so soon."

"I ...I ..." she stuttered but refused to look at him.

"What did I do? At least tell me what I did wrong that made you change towards me. You stopped speaking to me. It was almost as if you hated everything about me suddenly. It hurt me!" Lloyd inquired, he couldn't hide the pain in his voice, and he wanted answers.

"I didn't think I have that much effect over you to hurt you," she said softly, finally looking at his eyes.

Raising a hand to the hard lines on his face, down to his lower lip, she sighed. "WE can talk about this later. For now, I think you should rest."

"No" He shook his head and held her closer. "Tell me the reason now. I can hear your heartbeat; your cheek is flushed, and your eyes are telling me that you want me. So why are you pulling away from me?"

Felicia's hand dropped to her side, and she pulled out of his hold. "I have to go now" she didn't wait to hear or see his reaction; she picked up the plate and literally ran out of the room.

He closed his eyes and ran his fingers through his hair in frustration as he fell back against the bed. Felicia can run all she wants, but she would be his, and he would find out the reason for the fear in her eyes.

***

Felicia just laid back in bed but didn't sleep. She couldn't sleep at one point in the day. She had realized that she had forgotten her birthday and today was actually her birthday.

So, she went online to check up on Francisca and saw the big party organized for her. It was as if the whole family had moved on from her, and no one remembered her. Even though her fake death was just three months old.

After feeling blue about herself for a few hours, she checked up on Lloyd and saw that he was on his feet. She stepped out of the house and went to *the undead*. It was a friendly club that opened in the morning. Felicia sat with, her back hunched slightly over the table as she tried to not break down in tears. No one would ever understand how much self-control it took her to sit there, drinking a glass of margarita when all she wanted to do was throw a tantrum howl at the universe.

This was supposed to be her happiest day as one only got to celebrate their birthday once in a year, but here she was, having a fucking drink by herself and wallowing in self-pity.

"Do you need anything else, ma'am?" the server asked, bending her head slightly so she won't miss Felicia's reply as the bar was buzzing with activities and people.

Felicia shook her head, waving her off. She's had enough drink for one day and wasn't planning on getting drunk out here alone.

She clenched her fist as anger mingled with exasperation. The clock was ticking, and soon, her birthday would be over, but the thing is, she won't ever forget that it wasn't how she wanted it. Last year, she envisioned a large party, a big cake, and special treatment. Phew! Life wasn't fair.

Felicia had left the house a minute after 6 pm when she couldn't sit still after waiting for her father to call with a surprise, but he didn't. She had wished that Felix would call or send her a message all-day. She was twenty-five, and she would say that she wasn't the type of person who got envious of other people and that she shouldn't care about little things like this but after seeing the video of her twin on social media.

Laughing and jubilating on their birthday. A pang of jealousy that she had never felt before came over her. Yes, she knew that she was in protective custody, and everyone thought that she was dead, but that didn't stop her feelings from getting hurt.

She just wanted her day to be perfect, with the thrills of turning a year older and the happy tears of feeling loved, but no, none of that happened. There were no calls, no text messages, no surprises.

She had been in hiding for three months, and a birthday wish from her dad would have been the greatest consolation today.

A heaviness settled in Felicia's heart as the bar owner introduced a female singer to entertain the patrons. She wanted this to be about her; she wanted someone to call her up the stage and sing a birthday song for her, not some female in a lacey blouse that did nothing to conceal her perky tits and flat stomach singing about Love and some crap.

A picture of Lloyd flashed through her mind, but she dismissive it. Felicia's anger skyrocketed when the crowd cheered and erupted with applause as the female introduced her second song. She moistened her lips and held the microphone with her glove hands, her heads tipped backward as she blared the lyrics to ***Someone to Love.*** Felicia closed her eyes, imagining bright colors and dancing stars. She felt exposed, naked as the singer droned on, oblivious to the effect her music was having on Felicia.

Breath, Felicia

She did, her eyes moistened with tears as she pushed picked up the glass and gulped down its content, wincing Slightly as the effect hit the back of her throat. She waited for the usual calm that comes with drinking to envelop her heart, but nothing happened; instead, all she heard was her heartbreaking as she spotted a couple sitting at the far end corner of the room, the lady giggling at something the man was saying. Felicia looked away, willing her heart to stop beating so hard. Tomorrow, she'll pick up from where she stopped, move on like life wasn't unfair, and the world wasn't against her.

She could go to the spa or visit the cinema to watch her favorite movie. She could do all of these, but the thrill of doing it with someone or having someone do it for her was what she craved. She had worked her ass off throughout the years; her mind had painted different scenarios. She had made plans and had jotted them down in her notepad. None of which prepared her for a lone day at the bar, with a wild crowd that didn't match her state of mind.

The next set was a group of guys with tattoos and several body piercings. She cringed inwardly as the one that looked to be the leader took his lips between his teeth, pulling the lip ring into his mouth. The crowd roared, screaming their name.

Damn!

She swore silently as a guy almost bumped into her. He turned and apologized, his gaze lingering at her face. When she glowered at him, he scampered away, muttering incoherently under his breath.

As the band's voice echoed through the room, Felicia waved the server over and ordered another glass of drink.

"Here you go" the server placed the drink in front of her then stood for a best gazing at her with pity. Yeah, there was no logical explanation for a young lady as beautiful as Felicia sitting alone in a bar and having a drink all by herself. She had rudely waved off male attention as she didn't want anyone trying to weave a way into her pants. She had no patience for a man at that moment.

"What, you pitying me right now?" She snapped at the server.

The younger woman shook her head and made to talk, but the look in Felicia's eyes communicated her displeasure. She scrambled away, pushing through the crowd that was pulsating with energy and gusto.

Her phone buzzed with an incoming message; she ignored it, pushing it away from her. She didn't want to talk to anybody. She was the calm-headed twin, not. Francisco. So why was he acting like a baby who had you taken away? Fine, she hadn't made any plans because no one really knew her in New York, and she couldn't get her face on the internet because her life was still in danger from the Wedding psychopath.

But that still didn't make her feel alighted *all these feelings to hell!*

Her phone buzzed again, this time severally, and with such urgency, she was forced to check what the hell was going on.

She swiped at the screen; there were many notifications from one person. Lloyd!

The first one was 15 minutes ago. Ms. Smith, *where are you?*

The second one was immediately after, telling her to come

home.

Home

She sighed at the word. That was a damn apartment with fucking pieces of furniture and a few of her stuff. That wasn't home. Her home was in London with her family members. Not here in New York with a stranger!

Felicia knew that she was being a brat, but she couldn't stop how she felt for the life of her.

She scrolled through, deleting the notifications as her eyes searched for the one that was sent a minute ago.

Lloyd: *Please come home, Babe*

For a dozen beats, her heart skipped. Lloyd has never been one to say beg for any reason. Even when she stopped talking to him after their trip to Soho, he hadn't begged her; instead, he had asked her why she changed and when she hadn't replied to him. He backed off.

She debated whether to go home or not. While she was processing the notion of Lloyd being in trouble, her phone beeped again. She glanced at it without touching it;

Lloyd: *tell me where you are, and I'll come to get you*

Felicia heaved a sigh as she pushed up from the table. She decided to go for a ride first before heading to the apartment. It was just a minute past 8 pm, and the night air would do her some good. She dropped enough money to cover her drinks and a huge tip for the server, then made her way to the front door, pushing through the crowd that had increased in the last few minutes. The DJ had taken over the stage, and the dance floor was jam-packed with sweaty bodies, hence, the nauseous smell of cheap cologne and aftershave.

"Sorry, doll!" A man yelled after he almost shoved her down in his haste to catch up with his friends that were entering the bar

Felicia exhaled slowly, wishing the cool breeze would help soothe her nerves tethering on edge. She felt utterly drained as she had spent the last five hours hating on everything except the drink that had helped calm her.

She opened the door to her car and slid into the driver's seat, relaxing her back on the cold leather seat. She ignited the car, winding down the window to let in the night air. With a smile that didn't quite reach her eyes, she reversed into the dimly lit streets, turning off the radio as she wanted the only sound to be the one in her head. You are pushing Lloyd away from you when he did nothing to deserve it.

Her phone vibrated with an incoming call.

Lloyd.

She sent it to voicemail and reversed into the street to take her to the apartment instead. She pushed opened the door and met the room dark, no sign of him. She checked the kitchen, then the balcony. The bedroom was her last bet; Lloyd lied to sit there and watch people walk by. Felicia assumes that it was because he was a police officer, and he felt more comfortable knowing who was coming and going.

The door leading to the hallway was locked. Was this some kind of joke? She racked her brain, searching for any news about people being attacked in their homes, but came up empty, except......

The door opened, interrupting her thoughts. Lloyd stood there, dressed in his casual clothes. The first four buttons on his shirt were undone. Felicia felt it was intentional on Lloyd's part. He knew pretty well what his chest does to her senses.

"What the hell was so important that you wouldn't let me have a drink in peace, Lloyd?" she barked at him, her eyes bright with fury.

"I came home, and I didn't see you. So, I was worried. And you didn't mention going out today" he paused and took a step closer to her, "are you alright?" He asked, his voice laced with concern that grated on her nerves

Bloody hell! A fucking babysitter? Really?

"Are you being serious right now, Lloyd? Do I look like a child to you? We haven't said more than six words in one standing to one another in the last two months, but you are acting as if we are on chummy terms."

Lloyd swallowed as the faint wave of her perfume wafted through him. All he wanted to do at that moment was take her in his arms and tell her how beautiful she looked, all fired up. "I'm sorry. I thought maybe...."

"Don't fucking repeat those stupid words, Lloyd. I'm not a child. I'm not your fucking responsibility!"

"But you are my responsibility. I am here to protect you!".

"I can take care of myself" Felicia pronounced each word so that Lloyd could hear her clearly.

"Have you had dinner? I could order something. What are you craving?" He smiled, " I could use French dipped sandwich right now," he added chirpily

"Did you hear a word I said?"

Lloyd nodded. "Sure, did, but I have no intention of fighting with you today."

"Why?" She scoffed, telling her eyes.

"Remember that I am not a pro," Lloyd said as he coughed lightly and took a deep breath. He opened his mouth and started singing the birthday song. Felicia didn't know where to cry or laugh. Her emotions were jumbled.

As he sang, he moved closer to her and wrapped his arms around her waist.

Felicia looked at him in surprise. "You knew? You knew today was my birthday?" Her voice shook with a sob

Lloyd stared at her pointedly. "When you are supposed to remember that I am a police officer, you forget, and when it would be preferable that you forget, that's when you remember."

He hugged her tightly, relishing in the feeling of her warm arms and the soothing Scent of her perfume that always calmed him and turned him on. Right at that moment, he could feel his dick straining against his pant. She must have felt it because she pushed him away, then crossed her arms across her chest

"Don't think that just a song is going to earn your way into my pants, roomie," she countered, rolling her eyes at him

Lloyd chuckled, " come on, I've got a surprise for you."

He held her right hand, walked her towards the bedroom, then slowly nudged the open door, watching her reaction. His heart went like a bat out of hell when she sucked in a breath, her eyes tearing up again.

Felicia's heartbeat kicked up a knot as she glanced around the room. Everything she wanted was lined up on the floor amidst the scented candles that were both soothing and sexy.

"How did you know?" She asked him, her voice barely above a whisper

He shrugged, his eyes scrutinizing the room as he searched for the best way to tell her; he went snooping around her pieces of stuff and came across her notepad, and her wish to make her birthday special

He settled for the truth and almost jumped up with joy when she didn't get mad at him. Instead, her eyes warmed a fraction as she picked up the first box with the lingerie he had purchased from her favorite store

"Oh. My. God!" She breathed, "you didn't!"

He laughed, "it didn't walk here, Felicia."

She smiled before pulling it out. It was red. "Thank you"

Before he could say a word, she ran into the ensuite bathroom and closed the door. He thought she wanted to use the toilet, but when she emerged, his breath caught in his throat. She had gone in to change, and damn! She was sexy as hell; could probably make a dead man swoon

"Babe," he purred, uncaring about how his voice sounded deep with arousal. He could perceive his precum that was leaking onto his pant. God, he wanted her! But first, he needed to be sure she was doing this out of gratitude as tonight would be different. He planned on making love to her. Thoroughly. He was done playing around and pretending he didn't know her. Be the reason behind everything that concerns her

"I want to do this," she said as dark, sensual tension shuddered through her, her round curves pressing into him

"But the other..." He stammered, trying to be logical when his groin was screaming at him to just take her against the wall

She winked and giggled, brushing his hand lightly, "the gifts can wait."

She took his hands in hers and pressed them to her tits, "I want you to squeeze them," she cooed

Lloyd didn't wait for a second command. He palmed her tits, pinching her taut nipples, thereby eliciting a loud moan from her lips. She was beautiful. Even with her face devoid of makeup, she still knocked him out.

He kissed her shoulders blades, sucking gently as he didn't want to rush it. He wanted her to feel it all. He wanted her to remember tonight. God! He wanted her to love him.

With trembling hands, Felicia reached for the buttons on his White crisped shirts and frantically tore them open, sending the tiny buttons flying around the ground. She pushed the shirts off his shoulder, the same time he pulled out her tits, feasting hungrily on her nipples. Biting, sucking, kneading, taking.

She threw back her head and clasped his head closer to her, begging him to take her already.

He sucked on her reddened nipples, his fingers trailing downwards to her belly, then down to her pant line. He brought them back up, smiling when she bit his shoulder in frustration as her thighs were clamped together. He pushed his legs between her thighs and groaned when the wetness dripped from her center onto his thigh. "You're so wet," he moaned, moving his lips to her bellybutton

"Then fuck me already!" She whimpered as her pussy throbbed with an almost painful need, "Please, fuck me."

Lloyd winced at the word but ignored her pleas. He dragged the red underwear down with his teeth, nibbling lightly on her skin as the scent of her perfume mingled with the musk Scent of her arousal. He couldn't wait to put his mouth down there. So, he did. Kissing her pussy lips gently before pushing in his tongue

"You hungry, Felicia?" He asked while lapping on her sweet drip. It tasted like blueberry and a pint of apple.

"Yes! Yes Yes!! Right there!" She gyrated on his face

Energy pulsed. Breath quickened. Mouth agape.

She moaned, bouncing up and down his face as he tongue-fucked her pussy. His hands grabbed her ass cheeks as he spanked her lightly

"Don't stop."

Lloyd hummed a reply, then pushed in a finger, curving it slightly to meet her G-spot. She held onto his head tightly as pulsations rippled through her, sending her over the edge.

Lloyd led her to the bed and kissed her all over, his tongue lingering lightly over her breast and her sensitive parts. Then he pushed into her, filling her whole

Felicia sobbed as he moved slowly above her. This wasn't the fuck she demanded. He was making love to her, and for a split second, she felt the walls dropping as she thrust slowly into her. Her hips moved to meet his, heightening every stroke.

Skin tingled as the pleasure increased, and when he said the words, she looked away, avoiding his.

"I love you, Felicia," he repeated as his chest crushed her breast, his thrusts getting faster and slower. Torturing her

With one final Stroke, he exploded inside her, kissing her longingly. His tongue swiveling around hers as he said the words over and again

She didn't love him yet, but he was a patient man, and he was willing to wait for as long as it would take to make her see that he was more than just a quick fuck!

CHAPTER TEN

The incredible views of the East River, Manhattan Bridge, Brooklyn Bridge, and Brooklyn on the other side of East River while jogging would have been the best thing, but Felicia stopped and bent. Her hands were on her knees as she tried to catch her breath.

After leaving Lloyd at the house, she had changed into joggers and headed out for a quick run but ended up running more miles than she had earlier planned. There was a reason why Lloyd was the only man she avoided. He was the only man that turned her inside into pudding.

Yesterday she had broken her promise and almost made that wedding psychopath win because of her feelings for Lloyd, she was angry at herself, but she couldn't stop the way she felt when he was near her. In a weird sense, she felt complete in soul and body every time they were today.

She caught sight of some children fighting in an alley. A bigger older boy about sixteen and a younger skinny kid of about twelve. "Hey, stop that," she said, heading into the alley. She pulled both boys apart. "Will stop it, don't you know you can hurt one another?"

Maybe it was the smile on their face that gave them away, but when she saw the suspicious smile on the boy's faces, she knew that all was not what it seemed to be. She glanced at the path she had taken into the alley and knew that she was in trouble when she saw two rough-looking men in their twenties blocking the path.

They held their shirt high so that she could see the weapons under them. Instinctively she stepped back hastily, then turned around and broke into a run. The men ran after her, but Felicia was faster. As soon as she turned into a corner, she kicked a metal bin with all her might so that it went flying to the other end of the alley.

Then quickly, she hid behind some planks at the very beginning of the corner and covered herself with a large blanket type saw she saw hanging on a rod. Then she dialed Lloyd's number, it rang, but Lloyd didn't answer the call.

She sighed in despair because he could still be sleeping, and he could have turned his phone on silent to avoid disturbance. Suddenly, she heard the sound of approaching steps and curled into a ball, closing her eyes in prayer.

Please don't find me...please.

"Where did she go," A rough older voice asked angrily.

"Why are you asking me? We got here simultaneously," came the reply from another older voice.

Felicia heard the slap sound and knew that the man with the first voice had slapped the second man.

"Do I look like I cared? That woman smelled of money. We caught a big fish today, but you lost her," shouted the first voice.

"I think she went that way," the second voice stuttered.

Felicia closed her eyes tightly, praying that they would take the bait of the metal bin. It seems that her prayers were about to be answered when she heard their footstep walk beside where she hides. She heaves a sigh of relief.

At that moment, something crawled over her legs, and she yelped in fright, throwing the rag off her head. She realized a second too late, she started running away again but fell against a hard surface.

"Hey, baby," came the voice of the hard surface.

'Lloyd?" she looked into his non-smiling eyes and felt cold all of a sudden. Lloyd looked scary.

"Hey, leave," the first man called. "We caught her, so fuck off if you don't want any trouble

"But I like trouble," Lloyd snicked, grabbing Felicia's hand and pulling her behind him. "Despite how much I would love to fight you twats, I have other things to do, so I will give you both a suggestion, leave, and I would forget this ever happened, or you can face me."

"Let's get out of here," Felicia whispered. "They have knives and guns

"And I am a police officer," he assured her confidently.

The men who came after Lloyd, the first man who seemed to be the boss, got a flying kick that made him somersault and fall to the ground with a loud scream. The second man also ran towards Lloyd, rolling his hands at his side to create momentum for his punch, but Lloyd held him by the collar at the last minute and punched him in the face.

The man felt flat on his back. Lloyd turned around and faced her with a proud smirk on his face. "Told you I am a policeman."

"Yeah, you said" Felicia laughed at his exaggerated show of hands. "I called, but you didn't pick, but you got here as soon as if got into trouble."

"Something told me to go jogging when you went out this morning," He winked.

"I should be thankful for that something" Felicia ran and threw her hands around his neck. "Thank you"

"I should help you out of dangerous situations more" he laughed but suddenly groaned in pain.

"What? What happened" she pulled back and noticed that the first man on the floor had stuck a knife to Lloyd's back. "No, no, no, no!"

Felicia picked the rod beside her and swung it at the criminal. The surprise attack made him fall to the ground, unconscious. Felicia rushed back to his side, but he fell to the ground as she got to his side. She caught him last minute and pressed her hand on the wound.

"No! Why would this happen? You are fine, you are going to be okay!" she cried, moving her head back and forth. "I should call

911," she told herself.

Without reducing pressure, she removed one hand and pulled out her phone. The 911 call connected immediately. She didn't wait for the operator to speak. "Please come quickly," she cried heartbreakingly, rushing the words. "He is losing blood; he has been stabbed!"

Lloyd tapped her gently. "You have to slow down; the operator won't hear you clearly."

Felicia tried to calm her nerves by breathing deeply. "We are in a corner near the east river."

The operator told Felicia not to end the call. Felicia nodded the understanding forgetting that she wasn't on a video call.

"If I hadn't gone out. All this wouldn't have happened," she sniffled through her occasional hiccups.

"Don't say stuff like that," Lloyd groaned, holding Felicia's free hand. "Will you tell me why you hate me?"

"Hate? I can never hate you! I am stupid. I thought that if I dated you that I would be letting that wedding psychopath win, so I pushed you away even though you are the one I love the most in this world."

"You love me?" he asked in bewilderment. he turned on his side to look directly into her eyes. "I wish you told me; I wouldn't have had an easier time."

"Stop talking like that" she hiccups between words. "You keep talking as if you are about to die. Stop it! The ambulance will be here soon."

"If I die now, I would have no regret," he said, his eyes closing as he spoke.

Felicia shouted. "Lloyd Dean, don't you dare die on me. I won't forgive you."

Lloyd blinked and opened his eyes wild. "I won't die on you. I promise"

Felicia felt it before she saw it. His hands grew limps in hers and fell limply on his side. Felicia stared at him dazedly. Her mind refused to acknowledge the scene in front of her. She shook his shoulder with her free hand. "Please don't do this, Lloyd. I am begging you."

He didn't move. He was too still on the floor. Scenes like movies played before her eyes. When he had pleaded for a reason for her actions, she didn't reply. She had been more interested in punishing a psychopath than loving Lloyd.

The ambulance came, and the paramedic pulled Lloyd into a stretcher and headed for the ambulance. Felicia watched his limp body, and she couldn't believe that this was the energetic man she had lived with for the past two months.

He couldn't be dead because of her, or could he?

Wait? Why is the male paramedic shouting at her? Oh! It must be because she was falling to the ground, embracing the darkness around her. A smile spread across her face. She would be joining Lloyd soon…

CHAPTER ELEVEN

Felicia woke up, and the first face she saw was Lloyd. She threw her hands around his neck and cried in happiness. "I thought I lost you forever," She cried into his neck, hugging him tightly as if she thought he might leave if she let go.

"Felicia, I can't breathe," he chocked, tapping her arm around his neck.

"So, are we dead? This heaven" she glanced around the room quickly.

Lloyd smiled. "Why would you think that we are dead?"

"I saw you die," she sniffled but looked around her surrounding for the first time. She was sitting on a bed in the emergency ward with a drip attached to her hands and an IV pole beside Lloyd attached to his hand.

"You-" she pointed at him in shock. "I thought you were dead!"

Felicia jumped on him and threw her hands around his neck again. Lloyd smiled but groaned in pain, holding his lower abdomen. 'As you can see, I am very much alive," he assured.

The privacy partition curtain used to demarcate the ward was pulled aside suddenly, and Felicia caught herself staring into the eyes of a furious nurse.

"Are you trying to reopen your stitches" the brunette nurse glared at the two of them?

Felicia jumped away from Lloyd. "I am sorry, I was shocked. I didn't mean to hurt him."

"But are you trying to hurt yourself?" the nurse turned her

attention to Felicia, her hands on her waist; it was evident that she was trying hard to hold her anger in. "You hit your head hard when you fell two days ago, but you are jumping around instead of resting, and you, mister, in case you have forgotten, you were stabbed, and you were in surgery for six hours. Just because you are awake does not give you the right to move around."

Both Felicia and Lloyd glanced at one another with guilty expressions.

***

"Hello, dad? I promise I am fine!" Felicia assured her father for the umpteenth time. She was sitting on the bench outside the hospital. A nurse had advised that she take the call outside.

"Are you sure?" Felix's concerned voice came over the line.

"Why don't you believe me? Do you think that I would lie to you?" she asked calmly

"So, you are sure Lloyd is the only one who got hurt?"

"Yes!"

"You don't have to raise your voice. I wanted to be sure," he reprimanded.

Felicia let out a sigh. "Dad, I am not a baby. I am twenty-five; there is no need to lie to you. If I was hurt, I would tell, so stop asking me the same question over and over."

There was a short pause on the other end of the line. "You sound different, more confident. I like it, and you also sound angry."

"I-I…"

Felicia wanted to say that she wasn't angry, but that would be a lie. Her birthday was some days ago, and he still hadn't wished her even though it was too late.

"Was it about your birthday? Are you angry?"

Felicia shook her head. "No"

On the other end of the line, you could hear Felix chuckling light, then he coughed lightly as if he had something to say.

"The one thing you have never been able to hide is your jealousy."

"I am not jealous," I snapped loudly.

"You are right, baby girl," He answered sarcastically. "But I didn't plan Francisca's birthday; her husband did. I was swarmed with work and seeing the commissioner, among other things. I didn't even notice the date."

"So, you are saying that you haven't wished any one of us a happy birthday yet?"

"Yes, actually" Felix's voice held some mischief. "So, happy birthday, my baby girl. I am glad and thankful to God that you and your sister are alive and see how you have grown confidently over the last few months. I am proud of you."

"Dad…You are making me shy" Felicia was telling the truth; her whole face was red.

Somehow, hearing her father call her confident made her heart swell with pride, and she suddenly felt like she could walk on a cloud. Those few words pleased her more than she would like to admit. "I love you, dad," Felicia said quietly

"I love you more, darling."

The line on the other end beep that the call has ended. Felicia smiled to herself. Her father might be patient, friendly- sometimes and all-around dependable but he was a cut to chase kind of person. He had delivered the information he wanted to pass and get the information he wanted. Every other thing was extra.

"Fran?" a soft voice said loudly behind Felicia.

Instinctively Felicia turned, if she had taken an extra second to think about it, maybe she wouldn't have, but it was a twin thing, even as young children. If someone called a wrong name, the twins would still answer even if it wasn't their name because the person might not have been able to tell the twin apart.

The first thing that came to Felicia's mind after turning was that she should run because this person likely knew her sister, but she would look more suspicious if she ran.

"I thought you said you couldn't travel because you were pregnant, but you are in New York?" the young woman continued, her voice laced with surprise despite her words.

Is Fran pregnant? A smile spread over Felicia's face when she thought of how her sister would look pregnant. She resisted the sudden urge to ask the woman but stopped herself. With grim determination, she turned her smile into a frown and raised her brow.

"Do I know you, lady? "Felicia asked in her most dismissive voice.

"What? Is this some sort of joke?" a hint of anger was in her voice now. "It's Claire, your roommate!"

"First of all," she sighed. "I don't know you or any Flare or Fran, so leave me alone. I am trying to enjoy the night air."

Felicia brushed past the woman and started walking towards the hospital sliding doors, but Claire caught up with Felicia grabbing her hand.

"I can't believe it; you do look like her, but you don't sound anything like her," Claire apologized

Felicia pulled her hand from Claire's hold. "I have a ubiquitous face; you must have mistaken me for some, you know."

"I am sorry" she bent slightly.

Felicia nodded and continued walking back to the hospital door. It took a lot of willpower not to break into a run, but she did it. As soon as the door closed, she rested behind a pillar as her leg gave out under her. Felicia let out the breath she hadn't realized that she was holding.

"That was close," she breathed loudly, holding her chest. She should better tell Lloyd what just happened

***

"Hello" Francisca picked up the phone but didn't hear anyone on the other end of the line. This has been happening for a while, but she was more irked by it tonight.

There was silence on the other end of the line. Francisca blew a raspberry, took the phone from her ear, and was about to hang up the call when she heard the faint voice on the other end.

"Hello, Fran?"

"Claire?" Francisca was surprised but happy to hear her friend's voice. "It's been a while."

"It has, but that's not the reason I called," Claire said excitedly. "I saw something that looked exactly like you today."

"I don't understand...."

Clair didn't hear the edge in Francisca's voice as she continued describing the incident.

"And you thought that I was the one?"

"Well, after speaking to the woman for a few seconds, I realized how wrong I was. It must have been Felicia!"

"Claire!" Francisca thundered, pacing around a spot with her hands tightened into a fist. "Don't you dare say her name; must you do this? I am just getting over her death, and you play a stunt like this"

"I am sorry," Claire apologized frantically. "I didn't mean to cause you any type of pain. I swear that this woman looked like you to the latter, which confused me. I really thought that she was you...."

"Stop it!" Francisca interrupted. "I don't want to hear another word"

"I am so sorry. I won't talk about her anymore. I came to New York for some business. I will give you a call when I come to London."

"Huh-uh"

Claire seemed to slap her mouth. "This mouth of mine, but If not for a few scar injuries on her face, I would have called you the same...."

"You are still talking."

"I will shut up now. Bye."

The line went dead after the bye, and Francisca gently settled on the couch behind her. She could feel the bitterness coming up her throat and didn't like the feeling.

It has been months since she lost her twin, and she wasn't over yet. She hadn't attended the funeral before she was in intensive care, and Felix didn't wait for her to get better before he organized one.

Everything had happened so fast that she didn't want to accept the reality of her situation, but she was seeing psychiatrists remind her that Felicia was dead, but Clair said that she saw their lookalike in a hospital.

Francisca didn't want to think about it, but her brain was already on a full gas pedal mode. It was a popular troupe; a character could lose their memories after a traumatic experience in a movie or story. Francisca's eyes grew large as she started to put two and two together.

First and foremost, Felicia was in a car accident, and if she had survived, it would have been so traumatic that she could have blocked out the memory.

Also, didn't Claire talk about scars? Only superman would have walked away from that incident without a scratch, so Felicia needs to have scars if she is alive. Third and finally, the closed coffin. No one had seen Felicia's dead body because the family wanted privacy!

Francisca stood up fast. A little too fast because her head felt like it was spinning as soon as she got to her feet. She felt a strong hand around her, catching her. The young woman didn't have to turn around to know that she was in her father's arms.

Francisca spent the weekend with her parent while Charles traveled out of the country for a business trip. He said he didn't want his pregnant wife roaming around the house alone.

"Dad, I found proof this time," Francisca said breathlessly.

"Truth?" Felix helped Francisca back into her chair. "You need to rest. Don't you see that you are carrying the grandchild of this family?"

If Felicia wasn't so tired, she would have laughed. "Dad?"

"Huh?"

"Felicia is in New York, and she is alive," Francisca answered suddenly.

Felix's hands around Francisca tense, and he swallowed hard. His head went blank, and he could feel himself shivering.

"What did you say?" His voice was a bit above a whisper.

"My friend saw Felicia, dad. She is very much alive!"

"I think you don't know what you are saying" Felix gently lays Francisca back on the chair. "I am coming."

Felix didn't know how he met himself outside the house. His hand shaking as he opened his car door and slid inside. Once inside the car, Felix tried to think. How did Francisca find out? He shouldn't be thinking about that right now. If Francisca can find out where Felicia is, that psychopath could also find out where his daughter is and kill her. He gripped his steering wheel as sweat beaded on his forehead.

Is he going to move to have to move Felicia to another country again?

CHAPTER TWELVE

Lloyd didn't come home for another week, and visitation was restricted. The doctors claimed that he was always hurting himself whenever he saw his guest- she. Felicia growled to herself. What do those doctors know? The fact that Lloyd saw her every day was why he had a speedy recovery.

Felicia decided that since Lloyd would be back tomorrow, she could do some house cleaning and cook something for him. She couldn't cook anything except fry egg, make toast, wraps, and ramen. Once upon a time, she had considered that enough cooking skills, but now she knew better.

Having woken up early, she had cleaned the whole house from top to bottom. Now it was eight p.m. Friday night, and She was focusing on a YouTube channel, but the only thing she understood was the recipes. Finally, she decided it would be better if she didn't give a recently discharged patient poison to eat because she would be making for him. She closed her YouTube page and sank to the kitchen chair.

The sound of the doorbell ringing got her off her seat as soon as she sat. She looked into the peephole and saw Andrew. She smiled. The young man had taken it upon himself to deliver groceries after Lloyd's accident. He was too good for his own good.

"You are a lifesaver, Andrew," she said as she opened the door.

Andrew fell through the door as soon as she opened the door. Shocked, she caught him before he touched the ground. There was a big bump on Andrew's head.

"And from the dead, she shall rise!" A menacing voice said above her.

Felicia stared over Andrew's unconscious body to see a lanky man in his late twenties smiling at her. "Who are you, and what have you done to Andrew?" Felicia tried to keep her voice steady, but it broke nevertheless. The man was smiling while holding a knife!

"Did you cut him?" Felicia couldn't hide the fear in her voice anymore.

"No" The man bit his lips and squatted in front of her so that he was on the same eye level as her. "I wanted to use the knife, but instead, I used your fire extinguisher."

The man tapped Andrew on the head. "What a lucky fellow"

"I will call the cops if you don't leave right now."

The man suddenly started laughing, holding his side as the laughter wracked his whole body.

"Call them, please call them. Do you even know how I am?" he clicked his cheek like an excited baby. "I am-"

"The wedding psychopath" Felicia just knew he was the one.

"You are so smart," he clapped excitedly. "Maybe I won't kill you. No, I am definitely going to kill you. I mean, you had all the time in the world to get married, but you didn't. weren't you scared of what I would do to you?"

Felicia was scared of the murderer in front of her, but he was more pissed. This was the asshole who wrecked all of their lives. Felicia headbutted him and ran up the stairs; once she got up the stairs, she realized that her phone was still in the kitchen and he couldn't call the police.

Felicia heard the loud bang of the door closing shut and knew that he was alone in the house with a mad man. She slipped into the closet and closed the door.

"Come out, come out where ever you are, "the man said in a sing-song voice.

The door to the closet opened, and the mad man shouted. "Peek a boo" before hitting her with the barrel of a gun.

***

The next time Felicia would wake, she found herself tied to one of the kitchen chairs. The crazy man was watching videos on her phone. First, she tried to get out of the ropes, but she couldn't. It was too tight.

The chair creaked under her weight.

"About time you woke up," he said, looking up from her phone as she walked over to squat in front of again. "You know that all girls are the same, especially the rich ones, always thinking that they you are better than everyone else."

"But I didn't do anything to you," she shouted angrily.

"Call me Dwayne," he said, placing the sharp side of the knife beside her face. "If you scream again. I will gut him and peel off your skin from your face."

Felicia folded her lips tightly shut. Andrew was on the floor, still unconscious by the kitchen entrance. Indirectly he had gotten into trouble because of her. She wished with all her heart that he was fine.

"Do you love him? Wait, how many people are you sleeping with?" he licked the knife slightly, cutting his tongue. "I don't understand you. Andrew is not rich; Lloyd's family is well off, but you can do better. I mean, your family is practically royalty."

Felicia didn't say a word.

"I need to make you people understand your place. You are a woman. You need to fucking learn respect!" he slapped her across the face, bursting her lips.

He rubbed her face gently, and Felicia tried to stay still and not yelp in pain, but it was hard.

"Please let me go," she begged!

"I also want to let you go, but I can play favoritism. You were the fourth person I should have killed, but you made it go wrong, but now I have to fix it-"

"What are you saying?" Felicia cried.

Dwayne never finished his explanation as Lloyd appeared out of nowhere and swung a fire extinguisher over his head. The man fell limply to the ground, but Lloyd spun him around and planted his fist in the mad man's face.

'I have always wanted to do that when I found you," Lloyd muttered as he stood up from the now incapacitated psycho. Turning, he faced a frightened Felicia whose face was filled with tears. "Babe, are you okay?"

The front door crashed into the room as police officers swam into the room holding guns and shields. The officer in front who seemed to have led the operation sighed relief when he saw that everyone was fine.

"We came a little late, huh?" the commanding officer joked

"Lloyd untied the rope around her arms and legs; as soon as she was released, she fell into his arms, crying. He patted her back gently.

"You are safe now. It is over" he hugged her trembling body to his. "He has been caught"

As Felicia wrapped her hands around Lloyd's, she noticed that Dwayne was coming to; she pulled out of Lloyd's embrace and stood over Dwayne.

"Don't move," she warned, but he tried to stand up. Suddenly she kicked him in the ribs and bent in front of him "why won't you listen? I said, don't move!"

***

The police led Dwayne out to the cruiser for a free ride to the police station. The commander warned Felicia and told her that she would be arrested if she did it next time. Like a good child, she had nodded silently while he spoke, but she knew that if for any reason she set her eyes on Dwayne again, she would likely commit murder.

"Do you know why someone would do something as crazy as this?" Felicia asked.

Lloyd's hands were wrapped around her waiter as they both stared at the cruiser and ambulance leaving the house. The ambulance had carried Andrew to the hospital.

"An obsessed prick?" came Lloyd's reply.

Lloyd explained that Dwayne had been obsessed with a girl...

CHAPTER THIRTEEN

THREE YEARS AGO

Dwayne peeped from behind the pillar. He couldn't believe that anyone could be this beautiful. Jane, that was her name. She was twenty-four, working as an intern in a firm from a wealthy family. She was practically royalty, and he was in love with her.

His smile broadened when he saw when Jane saw the flowers in front of her car, but his smile disappeared when he saw her frown, and she threw the flowers away in anger.

Didn't she like the flowers? They were the most expensive kind, so what's not to like. He stormed over to her.

"Why?"

Jane took a step back away from him, her lips shaking when she Dwayne. "Stay away from me."

Dwayne was mad. "Why? I have told you a thousand times over that I love you. What is wrong with me? I am a good, hardworking man. I am handsome, and I got you flowers!"

"I am begging you, stay away from me!" Jane continued walking away from him.

"Okay, wait a minute. I am sorry" Dwayne realized that he was shouting at her, so he took a deep breath to calm his nerves. "I just wanted you to know that I love you, and I can see that you love me too."

Jane stumbled on a log behind her and fell on her hand. Dwayne rushes over to help her, but she pushes his hand away. He growled at her, raising his hand to strike her.

"Is everything fine here?" a voice asked.

Dwayne turned around to see a well-dressed man walking over to them in a tuxedo.

"We are fine," Dwayne answered quickly, lowering his hand.

"No, I am not," Jane told the man in fear, standing quickly, running, and hiding behind the man.

"It is a lovers quarrel. Don't mind her," Dwayne said gently. Trying to deescalate the situation. "You can leave; we will settle it ourselves."

"He is lying. I don't know him. He keeps stalking me. Giving me gifts that I never asked him for, and he gets mad when I tell him to stop!" Jane explained quickly.

The man in a tuxedo turned and faced Dwayne. "I will take this woman out of here, and if you dare follow us. I will call the cops and report you for stalking and harassment."

"I-" Dwayne started walking over to them but stopped. A woman had reported him for stalking last month, but the cops hadn't been able to prove anything. If this man reported him for stalking Jane, the police wouldn't sit still.

Dwayne clenched his fist tightly as he watched the love of his life. Why was Jane leaving with another man? Can she see his heart? Or did she think that he was not serious about her?

That was it! Jane thought he was not serious, and that was why she wasn't giving him the time of day.

He smiled to himself. He had the best idea to prove himself to Jane.

***

No! This wasn't how it was supposed to happen. Why was everyone laughing and taking pictures? Was it his fault that he fell in love with Jane? Bile rose in his throat as he stared at her face. There was no remorse in her eyes.

Dwayne could taste the peach drink on his face. He was soaked in it. When he found out that today was Jane's birthday, he got a big cake and ring. Then he went on one knee in the middle of the party.

Taking a deep breath. "Will you marry me, Jane, and make me the luckiest man in the world!"

As soon as Jane saw Dwayne on his kneel, she screamed rushes at him, tearing at his face with her fingers; the cake fell out of Dwayne's hand and fell to the ground in front of him.

Her friends had tried to pull her away from him, and they had succeeded, but Jane grabbed a glass of peach from passerby and threw it in his face.

"Get out, can't you just leave me alone and get out of here!" she screamed.

"I love you; can't you see that?" Dwayne cried like a baby. "I have proven that I would be a good man for you, so what do you want?"

Jane shrugged out of her friend's hold and slowly walked up to Dwayne; she continuously poked his chest with her finger. "Listen and listen good because I won't repeat this" her face and voice were cold. "I hate your eyes; the way you look at me gives me the creeps. You are ugly and poor with a horrible stench. If, for any reason, you were the only man in the world. I would still never have anything to do with you!"

Oh! The crowd exclaimed, but Jane wasn't done.

"You are poor, and I am rich, don't you see that we can't relate? And besides that, I begged you to stop, but you are so delusional that you thought that my being nice to you was because I had a feeling for you!"

Dwayne tasted the tears before he realized that he was crying. He glanced around the room and saw everyone laughing at him. He couldn't believe it. How can this happen? All he did was show her how he truly felt, and she looked down on him.

He couldn't believe that he could hate anyone, the way he hated jane at that moment. His father was right. Women needed to know their places. If Jane knew her place, she wouldn't disrespect him like this!

It was her fault. She seduced him, and when he showed her how he also felt. She made a mockery of his feelings.

He lowered his head and leaned beside her ear. "Remember this, you will pay with your life for this!"

Jane stepped away from him in fear, and he laughed. Yes! That was how she was supposed to feel when she saw him coming. Scared!

***

Two months later, when Jane was found dead. Of course, Dwayne was the first suspect, but he wasn't in the state at that time, so he was vindicated.

The police did not know that Dwayne had hiked a ride with a truck driver at that time. Slipped into town in the cover of night and killed Jane. After killing her, he had left the same way he came, and nobody knew he was the killer.

After killing Jane, the thrill Dwayne felt was something he had never felt before. It was a different kind of high, and he loved it. Then he heard that Jane's sister was getting married because their parent was scared to die without having a child.

Ironically that made Dwayne think he was some kind of God sent to teach Rich girls a lesson. So, like a god, he judged the women who broke his rule.

CHAPTER FOURTEEN

Felicia was surprised to hear the reason for her family's trauma was because a man got turned down by a woman. The excuse was so flimsy that she almost couldn't believe it.

But she still didn't know how Dwayne found out that she was alive. She was sure that she had followed every rule and regulation the police had given her to the latter.

Lloyd filled her on the reason while hugging her. When Claire saw Felicia a week ago, she had Fran tell her that she saw her look alike. Dwayne still wiretapped Fran's phone, and that was how he had put two and two together to figure out that Felicia was the girl Claire had met and the rest was history.

"I think that I should be the one to inform my parents that Dwayne has been caught, "Felicia told Lloyd.

"Your dad is in New York; let's give him the news when he gets here."

"Huh?" Felicia blinked in shock.

"Your dad suspected that Dwayne would follow you to New York after he found that Claire saw you, so he came himself to make sure he was wrong," Lloyd explained.

Felicia smiled at her father's thoughtfulness, but a tear also fell down her face. This year had shown her how precious she was to her father, and it made her heart full.

Felicia picked up the phone and dialed her father's number despite Lloyd's words. As soon as the call went through. Felix picked up the call.

"Hello, Felicia, are you okay?" Felix asked.

Felicia chuckled. "Yes, dad and the police caught the Wedding psychopath, and he is never ever going to hurt anyone ever again."

Felix sounded shocked, overwhelmed, and relieved. He cried like a baby when Felicia recounted the whole incident, how Dwayne attacked her and how he got caught. Felicia heard her father cry over the phone for the first time in forever.

"You don't know how thankful I am that all of this is over," Felix cried.

Felicia cried with him, but when Felix said he was coming over. She told him not to. Felicia had some things to take care of. Tomorrow she would see her father.

She hanged the call and watched as Lloyd went to pick up the front door that was broken down earlier. She knew she had forgotten something. So, she dialed another number that she knew by heart.

"Hello," Francisca's voice came in calmly.

"Hello Fran," Felicia said gently.

For a few seconds, Felicia didn't hear Francisca's voice. For a second, Felicia was sure that shocked her sister into fainting.

"Can you hear me, Fran? It is Felicia. I am alive. It is a long story, but I am alive."

Still silence.

Then Felicia heard Felicia scream. "Mom! I think I am really going crazy now."

Felicia chuckled through a face full of tears, but she was too happy to the car. She could hear sounds of hurried footsteps and Francisca's voice telling their mother to talk to the person on the phone.

"Hello, "Chloe said weakly into the phone.

"Mom, before you freak out. No, I am not dead. I didn't die; it was a long story. I have been in protective custody for a few months, and I am not dead, and we caught the wedding psychopath. He is behind bars!" Felicia said quickly, tumbling words together before her mother fainted, thinking she was talking to a ghost.

After a lot of coursing, Chloe finally believed Felicia. All three women cried and laughed on throughout the call. Chloe was not content with just hearing Felicia; she said they did a video call.

When Felicia switched to video call. The women cried again. Happy tears, Chloe said she would be on the next flight, but Felicia stopped her and told her mother that she would be back on the next available flight.

After a lot of cajoling, Chloe accepted, but she swore that she wouldn't forgive Felix for putting her in the dark; she was adamant that she was divorcing Felix after finding out that he kept everyone in the dark. It took the twins cajoling to convince her that divorce was too much of a punishment. Instead, she said she wouldn't forgive him for now.

Both sisters cried and spoke for an hour. With a heavy heart, Felicia finally ended the call.

Felicia finally looked up to find Lloyd looking at her, waiting for her patiently. She smiled for absolutely no reason; just looking at him made her smile.

Then she saw the scene around her, and the memory of what happened earlier came flooding through her brain.

"I don't want to stay here tonight," Felicia said.

"Me neither"

***

Felicia had never always been a sucker for art that was Fran's thing but here on top of the Museum of Arts and Design is Robert - a beautiful and elegant restaurant that overlooks Central Park and Columbus Circle, dressed simply in jeweled tones, she changed her mind. This was art, and it was beautiful!

Sitting on one of the chairs with Robert's exceptional cuisine in her hands, she couldn't think about food, but the only thing that mattered was the most beautiful art sitting right in front of her. After she told him that she didn't want to stay back at their place, he had suggested that they come to Central Park, and there they are.

"Felicia-" Lloyd reached over the table with his palm, and she held his hand. "I know you don't want to date because you don't want that madman to win."

He swallowed hard and stared her straight in the eye. "But you also told me that you loved me, fine, circumstances beyond our control put us together, but I can't think about a time without you in my life

"Lloyd, I -"

"Don't say no yet. I don't know how to beat about the bush. I have a real strong feeling for you, Felicia, and I need to know if you also feel the same about me."

"I do"

"Uh?" Lloyd's head jerked up in shock. "I don't understand; this is supposed to be hard, you were supposed to say no, and I was supposed to convince you that you were meant for me."

"No"

"Will you stop that?" Lloyd moans, raking his fingers through his hair, stressed. "I am serious right now, Felicia."

"So, I'm I " She shrugged and leaned across the table and planted a hot kiss on his lips. She started sitting, but Lloyd leaned against his and deepened the kiss. Finally, she pulled back and sat down. Her face flushed. "As I was saying. I am serious about you. When I saw you get stabbed, I realized how much I loved you and when I heard the reason Dwayne did those things. I was convinced that I wanted to spend my life with you. Dwayne was a sick man who had no control over his emotions and tried to force everyone into doing what he wanted"

"So, you mean?"

"I love you, Lloyd Dean."

"So, you mean you would like to marry me," he asked, picking each word gently.

"No," Felicia shook her head. This time she was sure that she saw a vein almost pop in Lloyd's neck. "First, that was not a proper proposal, and secondly, I want to know about your nightmares."

"You know about them?" his heart stalled for a split second.

She nodded. "You have been sleeping opposite my room for months now. Of course, I know about them. Can you tell me what happened?"

Lloyd sighed. "Last year, I had a partner, a female partner, and junior; she was good at her job and always tried to do what's right."

Felicia saw his body tremble and instantly regretted asking him to recount the experience. "You don't have to talk about it" she squeezed his hand.

"I want to," he squeezed back. "We caught a child trafficking ring; we had no backup; it was just the two of us. Her name is Diane McGinn. Earlier that day, she told me that she had just found out that she was pregnant and for her unborn baby, she wanted to make this ring pay" he laughed sadly. "We caught the ring alright, but then they caught some of the children and Diane. One of the sick bastards said if I didn't shoot her, he would kill the children."

"Lloyd, I am so sorry."

"Diane said she was fine, so I pulled the trigger and shot her on the thigh; the backup came after that. We saved the children, but Diane lost a lot of blood and the baby. After that, I couldn't hold a gun, and I got desk duty."

"I am sorry to hear that" she held her hand his hand tighter, trying to comfort him. "I am sure she didn't blame you."

"She didn't, but I blamed myself " Lloyd ran his hand over his face. "That was when the nightmares started; I took meds, but as time went by. I just got worse!"

"I am so sorry that you go through something as sad as this" Felicia didn't realize when the tears started falling down her face. "Together, we will work together to make your nightmares disappear."

He smiled, "You know what is funny, any time I am around you. I sleep peacefully anytime, with no nightmares. Just sunshine."

"Are you trying to say that I am your ray of sunshine?" Felicia couldn't stop blushing. She leaned and whispered into his ear. "I think we should get out of here; you are looking at me as if you want to eat me, and I can't control myself either."

Lloyd nods mischievously. "You are right; I think we should leave!"

Lloyd and Felicia didn't know how they left *Robert's,* but they knew it was on their own legs.

***

Back at the hotel, Felicia couldn't get enough of Lloyd as they nibbled and kissed one another; Lloyd covered Felicia's mouth with his and kissed her with every bit of love he felt. He pushed her against the door, holding her hands over her head with one hand while he pulled out the key card with another hand, kicking the door open.

As soon as the door opened, Felicia tore at his clothes, kissing and nibbling all around his chest, his ears, the hollow of his neck; she loved the way he trembled against her body. They fell on top of the bed in passion.

"Wait-" Lloyd pulled away from Felicia, putting distance between them

"What, why are we stopping again? Felicia asked breathlessly.

"You love me, right?"

"You are asking that now?" her eyes grew wide with shock.

He nodded. "Yes"

"I love you; I said that already. How many more times do you want me to say it" she said, throwing his arm around his neck and resuming kissing him.

"That's what I want to hear from you, "he said, kissing her back, holding her close. "I love you too, honey."

"Honey?" she asked, her voice filled with emotion. "Cool nickname, my Shakespeare. I love you too."

"Shakespeare?" He asked curiously.

Felicia smiled to herself. "It is a private joke," she said, snuggled against him.

He nibbled on her ear. "And you won't tell me?"

Smiling at him, she nodded and, as he pulled her back into his arm and fell back on the bed. Felicia knew in her heart that this was the place she would always want to be, right in his arms.

***

Lloyd stirred in his sleep when he heard his phone ring, the first place he looked at was at Felicia sleeping with her head on his chest. She groaned sheepishly, obviously disturbed by the ringing phone.

So, he grabbed the phone and reduced its volume, then slipped out of bed as quietly as possible. Walking on his tiptoe, hoping against hope that he wasn't making any noise. Once outside the bedroom, he glanced at his phone. It was a number he had never seen before; he slid up the answer button to answer the call.

"Hello?" Lloyd said, but it was more of a question.

"Lloyd?" A female voice asked.

"Yes, that's me."

"Guess what?"

Lloyd was baffled. First of all, he had no idea who was on the other end of the line, but the person was asking him to guess. To be honest, the voice sounded familiar, but he couldn't place it.

"Lloyd, are you there?" The voice asked; there was a lot of concern in her voice.

"Yes, I don't-"

"I am pregnant!"

Lloyd's eyes grew wider as realization hit him, and a broad smile grew on his lips. The name just rolled out of his lips without a doubt. "Diane McGinn!"

"The one and only. I found out last night. I told my husband, and I realized that there was one more person I wanted to share the news with, and that was you!"

Lloyd's tears fill with unshed tears. "You got a grown-ass man like me acting myself acting like a baby."

"I am always grateful that I met you; I wish you would stop beating yourself up" Diane sighed loudly. "Also, I am still the best partner you could ever ask for."

Lloyd couldn't stop himself from smiling; his cheeks hurt from happiness. After talking for a few more minutes, Diane said something about pregnant women needing extra sleep before ending the call.

When he slipped back into bed, Felicia wrapped her hands around him and snuggled deeper against him. A lightness settled in his chest because suddenly, everything seemed like it was coming together. Lloyd knew that tonight and every other night, he wouldn't be having nightmares anymore.

CHAPTER FIFTEEN

The Smith sisters become celebrities overnight. The tabloids published the news about the two sisters who lived after becoming a serial killer's target. Television stations wanted to interview them; everything changed in a blink of an eye.

Felicia hadn't found the right time to tell her parents that she was engaged or dating because they hardly let her out of the house and talked less of their sight.

Felicia and Francisca spent almost every minute together. It seemed to be the only thing that soothed Francisca. Francisco had woken Felicia up in the middle of the night more than four times. Francisca's calls were the same every day.

"Good morning, you are ok...hope you are fine. I just wanted to check up on you to see that you are still here," Francisca asked many nights.

Felicia didn't have time to date or see Lloyd. So, Lloyd told Felicia that she should inform him of the times her parent would be around because he would use that time to do something special. Felicia thought that Lloyd wanted to know the safe time to visit.

But now, Felicia opened her mouth wide and had to remind herself to close it. Lloyd was asking for her parents for permission.

"Good afternoon Mr. and Mrs. Smith. My name is Lloyd Dean. I am in love with your daughter, and I would love to marry her"

Felicia hadn't expected him to do that. She was both ecstatic and shocked. Even her parents were staring from Lloyd and back to her in shock.

"We, I," Felix stuttered; he looked lost too.

Chloe wasn't as shocked as Felix. Instead, she held his hand tightly. "You mean you love my Felicia?"

"Yes, ma," he nodded.

Chloe turned her face aside to see behind Lloyd and get a clear view of Felicia. "What do you have to say about this? Do you also love him?"

"Huh? I mean yes" Felicia quickly stood beside Lloyd, holding his hands, loving.

"You were asked to protect my daughter" Felix raised his brow. "No one thought you could try to steal her heart.

Felicia laughed nervously when she heard her father's voice; first, she was scared that Lloyd was about to be bashed with words. Lloyd removed his hand from hers and bowed his head gently.

"I am sorry that I acted unprofessionally when I was supposed to be protecting Felicia."

"I wasn't trying to make you sad or anything. I am just surprised, that's all" Felix looked angry.

Felicia looked from her man and back to her father. This was going horribly

She might not have known planned this meet but didn't realize that she wanted everything to go horribly wrong. Her mouth worked faster than her brain.

"He didn't seduce me. I liked him. So, I made a move on him!"

Felix kept staring at his daughter as if she had grown an extra head. After speaking with Lloyd, both parents accepted the proposition.

"If you love our daughter and she loves you too. Then we accepted; you have always been beside her from the beginning. So, it seems fair," Chloe said

Felicia jumped on him in excitement and threw her hands around his neck.

"I love you, Lloyd Dean," she cried

"And I love you too," he cried with her!

EPILOGUE

Claire stared around the office and let out a breath she hadn't realized she was holding. The office had a relaxed yet simple setting, it was the type of design that was meant to put people at ease and make them more comfortable, but something told her that people rarely feel that way when seated on this chair.

A female doctor stepped out from behind a cubicle curtain with a disarming smile and sat opposite Claire.

"Hello ma'am, I have your test results here," the doctor said calmly.

Claire's heart did a backflip, stopped beating, skipped, and resumed pumping blood back through her whole body in the space of seconds after hearing the doctor's words. Claire tried to force a smile, but she couldn't; she was on tenterhook.

She was sure she was wrong because it couldn't be, but there was no crime in getting professional advice. I mean, just because she started looking different does not mean that she can be pregnant. Right?

Just because her period hasn't started again this month doesn't mean she is pregnant. It could be caused by anything. I could be stressed. Yes, stress makes periods late on some people have their period late for two months, just like her right now.

Claire watched as the doctor opened the document, and suddenly she found her hands around the doctor's hands, stopping her from opening the document. Claire looked at the table and saw Doctor Gomez's name on the office name board.

"Doctor...Mrs, I mean Miss Gomez," Claire stuttered apologetically.

Doctor Gomez chuckled. "I am a Mrs, but that is beside the point" she took her hands off the table and documents. "I am getting the feeling that you don't want to know what is written in this document."

Claire nodded meekly without saying a word.

"But I hope you know that not looking at the test won't change your result," Gomez explained calmly.

"I know," Claire said with resignation, plopping down on the chair behind her, then ran her fingers through her hair and then rubbing her face with her palm. "It just doesn't make sense. None of this makes any sense."

"Okay, let us do this," Gomez says calmly. "Why are you here? Forget about the test. Just answer the question, why are you in the hospital."

Claire gulps hard. "I don't make sense."

"Try me"

"Okay," Claire sighs deeply. "I am certain that I haven't had sex with anyone, but I am pregnancy symptoms; I mean, my period was late for two months, and my body feels different, so I bought a pregnancy kit, and I tested myself-"

"So, what happened?"

"I bought like a dozen test kits, and they all have the same result. Al the result says that I am pregnant!" Claire's voice was close to screaming; she was losing her marbles. "So, I came to the hospital for a professional check-up because all that pregnancy test kit result has to be false."

"Well, Test kits don't always give a hundred percent result." Gomez said, "So, why don't I show you what a professional result says"

Claire nods and holds her breath as Gomez picks up the document again; she can't read the emotions on the doctor's face. Gomez had a perfect poker face on, and Claire couldn't tell what was going on in her mind.

Finally, Gomez places the paper on the table and smiles warmly.

"Claire? I can call you Claire, right?"

Claire nodded again but still kept her lips sealed. She stared at Gomez as if her life depended on o the doctor because it did!

"So, Claire, you know that being pregnant is not the end of the world."

"But, I can't be pregnant because I didn't sleep with anyone! I am a virgin!"

Gomez chuckles nervously. "But the test says that you are two months pregnant; maybe it was a day you cant remember. Is there a day in the last two months that you cant recall?"

Why hasn't she thought about it? It was that night that she went clubbing. That day that she cant remember. Did she? No, she couldn't have? Right?

Claire looked at Gomez with a plea in her eyes. " I couldn't have slept with a stranger and lost the memory, or can I? Could I" she looked at the doctor to refute what she just said, but somehow Claire knew that that wouldn't be the case!

About the Author

I am a hopeless romantic. Since childhood, I have always been interested in romantic tv series, novels, shows, etc. Also, I have been an avid reader since the age of 3. When everyone around me was busy playing, my comfort space had always been in books. When I was a teenager, instead of shopping and making new friends, I would happily make myself comfortable and dive into a book.

This is the reason why I decided to capture my imagination onto paper and begin my journey as a romance author. It is my hope that you will have enjoyed my unique romantic stories, and stay with me as I continue to pour my heart into my writing.

Free Gift

Sign up to my mailing list to receive an exclusive free novella, and be notified on any new releases, giveaways, contests, cover reveals and so much more!

https://dl.bookfunnel.com/kguy19f0uw

Is he just a holiday fling… or a soulmate beyond her wildest dreams?

My name is Olivia, and I've got no job, no partner, and nothing to look forward to. I could end it right there, but despite all of that, cupid works in mysterious ways.

When my girlfriends suggested a spontaneous trip to one of the most romantic cities on the planet, I could hardly refuse. The beautiful waterways of Venice might be hiding the man of my dreams… or at least they'll take my mind off my bad luck.

But I can't shake the feeling my friends are hiding something from me. I don't have much time to think about it – because now I find myself falling for someone, I never thought I would…

Is this nothing more than a holiday fling? Or could it blossom into something much more than I ever could have imagined? I guess there's only one way to find out.

Gear up for the fun and scintillating first book in the *LOVE & TRAVEL* series. Filled to the brim with wild emotion and romantic suspense, *Love In Venice* is an exciting love story that's guaranteed to give you your emotional fix.

www.ingramcontent.com/pod-product-compliance
Lightning Source LLC
Chambersburg PA
CBHW020454180726
47992CB00027B/2284